William T Hall

**The Turnover club**

Tales told at the meetings of the Turnover club, about actors and actresses

William T Hall

**The Turnover club**
*Tales told at the meetings of the Turnover club, about actors and actresses*

ISBN/EAN: 9783743328358

Manufactured in Europe, USA, Canada, Australia, Japa

Cover: Foto ©Andreas Hilbeck / pixelio.de

Manufactured and distributed by brebook publishing software (www.brebook.com)

William T Hall

**The Turnover club**

# THE

# TURNOVER CLUB.

TALES TOLD AT THE MEETINGS OF THE
TURNOVER CLUB, ABOUT ACTORS
AND ACTRESSES.

COMPILED AND WRITTEN BY

## "BIFF" HALL,

CHICAGO AND NEW YORK:
RAND, MCNALLY & COMPANY, PUBLISHERS.
1890.

THIS LITTLE VOLUME IS

AFFECTIONATELY DEDICATED TO THE

REPORTER'S BABY,

WHOM HE NICKNAMED "MISS PINKERTON"

SOON AFTER HER ARRIVAL IN THIS VALE OF TEARS.

WHEN ASKED WHY HE CALLED HER BY THAT

NAME, HE SENTENTIOUSLY REPLIED:

"WE NEVER SLEEP!"

# CONTENTS.

## V.

## VI.

## VII.

## VIII.

## IX.

## XIX.

## XX.

## XXI.

## XXII.

## XXIII.

12          CONTENTS.

## XXIV.

## XXV.

# THE TURNOVER CLUB.

## I.

There exists in Chicago a social club whose name is
not to be found in any telephone or city directory, though
its membership embraces the local master minds of several leading callings, and through its sessions it has given
to the world many well-turned quips and entertaining rem-
iniscences, which are the very antithesis of the dreaded
though bounteous "chestnut." This is the Turnover
Club. Its meetings are held weekly, in a well-known
down-town refectory. The hour is a matter of secondary
consideration; but the gavel usually falls when the "better classes" are wrapped in slumber. The sessions are
quite protracted, as no one member ever desires to with-
draw, for fear that his fellows may follow out the tenets
of the organization and tear pages from his own history,
to read them for the sake of idle curiosity and amusement.

The *personnel* of the Turnover Club, omitting names
and designating the various members according to their
respective callings, is as follows: The Proprietor, the
two Purveyors, the Manager, the Agent, the Actor, the

Professor, the Counsellor, the Night Clerk, and the Reporter—the latter reporting the proceedings of the weekly meetings for the official organ, the *Chicago Sunday Herald*. The Proprietor, whose shekels back the "Usual Resort" where the meetings are held, is looked upon as the organization's president, and the Purveyors, who stand directly in the rear of a couple of white aprons and cater to the assorted thirst of the members, are looked upon as the joint treasurers (or treasurers of "the joint") by general consent, securing, as they do, all of the available funds in the combined pockets of those whose names are upon the roster.

Ofttimes, when any one member of the Club finds his assets reduced to a pant-button and a solitary car-ticket, he is forced to commune secretly with one of the Purveyors. Upon these occasions their whispered colloquy is studded thickly with sibilant expressions, such as, "My tab," "To-morrow, sure," and "No change." If this subdued conversation results favorably to the member, he smiles blandly, and says, "This is with me," to the rest of the quorum; while the Purveyor makes an entry upon his elastic ledger.

A brief description of the members may not be amiss at this time. The Proprietor is a very dapper, natty individual, who prides himself upon the cut of his raiment and his general personal appearance. He affects the latest agonies in attire, and the glitter of the dainty dew-drop upon his rich scarf is like unto the sparkle in the eye of a Spanish señorita. He is well informed upon all current topics, and is loquacious to a degree. The Purveyors are exaggerated counterparts of their superior. Their attire is much more pronounced, and their scarfs more boisterous; their diamonds, too, are of greater diameter, circumference, and brilliancy, though the clouds of distrust lower darkly over their value as quoted by their owners. Though their abilities as analytical chemists are not known, their skill as compounders is acknowledged, and it is with proud mien and steady hand that either of them stands behind the polished mahogany and piles up the serried ranks of a *pousse cafe*, or dashes from glass to glass the highly colored ingredients of the enticing but delusive cocktail. In the ranks of the Club the Manager stands first and foremost, as he is usually the most solvent. As to dress and personal appearance, he is rather indifferent, probably for the reason that he is very near-sighted, and unable to closely examine what is foisted upon him by his tailor in the direction of habiliments. His overcoat is a barometer which invariably indicates his condition as to liquor: for, after every drink he takes, its collar approaches closer to his hat. He is the proud possessor of a laugh which never fails to greet the relation of one of his own anecdotes, and its cheery ring always rattles the bottles on the top shelf. The Actor, his menial and slave, wears a head of fiery red hair when off the stage, and is designated as a comedian before the foot-lights. The Agent, whose labors consist in heralding the approach of the Manager and the Actor in what he is pleased to term " jay towns," is a very talkative youth who arrays himself in gaudy attire, always appears beneath a newly ironed and shiny tile, and he spatters the atmosphere about him with the slang of the theater and "the road." As for the Reporter, he is a modest, unobtrusive young man, who seldom talks except in one of those mysterious conversations with the Purveyors, already referred to. He is a good listener, and is very fond of relating the achievements of his fellow members as personal experiences of his own. The other members—the Night Clerk, the Counsellor, and the Professor—well, they are entered to trot in the same class, and are never far away when the wire is reached.

*<br>* *

One evening last week the Club met, purely by accident, in the Usual Resort. One by one the members dropped in, the Reporter bringing up the rear on his way back from a "social event" out on California, just this side of Dubuque, Iowa. The Club leaned against the bar, put half of its feet on the nickel-plated railing, and the roll was called. The Proprietor rapped for order, and the Purveyor erased with a towel the liquid which was spilled out of the gavel in the operation. Under the call for unfinished business, the Reporter and the Purveyor held a whispered consultation, which did not appear to be satisfactory to either party. Finally the Reporter drew from its resting-place the Waterbury chronometer which had accompanied the suit of clothes he was wearing, and passed it over to the Purveyor. The latter placed it in the money-drawer, paying but little attention to the kiss thrown after it by its late owner, and turned back to the bar to receive the first order under the call of new business. This order was as follows: The Proprietor, "A little of the old stuff;" the Manager, "A gin fizz;" the Actor, "A Manhattan cocktail;" the Agent, "A John Collins;" the Professor, "Straight goods;" the Night Clerk, "Some of that Lithia water;" the Counsellor, "Sherry and egg;" the Reporter, "One beer;" and the Purveyor, "A dollar five, please." The order was disposed of by the following *viva voce* vote: The Proprietor, "Well, here she goes;" the Manager, "Here's looking at you;" the Actor, "Here's a go;" the Agent, "Swipes;" the Professor, "Happy days;" the Night Clerk, "Drink hearty;" the Counsellor, "Here's high

road to wealth;" the Reporter, "Gesundheit;" the Purveyor, "Thanks."

*.*
*

"Took in the minstrels to-night," said the Agent, as
he reached a cigar-lighter toward the Purveyor's Kohi-
noor, under the impression that it was the gas-jet on the
end of the bar. "Heard a joke that I first met with
Barnum in 1859—a respectable, hoary-headed fellow.
One of the end-men supported its tottering form, and led
it before the foot-lights in a manner that was truly affect-
ing. Reminded me of Daniel Bandman's first entrance
as *Lear*. By the way, I met Dan and his party last
month, when I was billing Tanksville, R. I. He is playing in dime museums now, along with the fat-headed
boy and the Albino princess. Plays *Richard III*. every
hour from one P. M. until ten P. M. Pretty tough on a
man to get killed nine times a day, I tell you. I guess
he's doing well. Only carries four people and one trunk.
His dime museum version of the tragedy only requires
three people, but he takes along an extra man in order
to get theatrical rates on railroads and at hotels. Then
he uses this man to play thinking parts, like the *Bleed-
ing Officer* and the two armies. He acts as a sort of a
bill-trunk, too, carrying all of the combination's printing
in his overcoat pocket. I dropped in to see the show
one rainy day. There was only fifty-five cents in the
house —one man bought a reserved seat. A fellow named
F. Tracy Booze plays *Richmond*. He's a professional
walker, and his railroad fare is saved on short distances.
They feature the combat scene—use hard gloves and
fight four rounds. The museum pianist accompanies
them. During the progress of the first round he plays
' Johnny, Get Your Gun ;' then he works the thing up
through ' See Saw' and 'White Wings' to 'Wait till the

2

Clouds Roll By,' after which *Richard* expires amid the sad, sad strains of 'Bid Me Good-bye and Go.' The show goes well."

*<br>* *

"I met our friend, Colonel Jack Haverly, to-night," remarked the Actor. "He's a hustler, and a sharp one, too. One of his 'Pompeys' was telling me of an experience Jack had with a member of the great English aristocracy. It appears that he was a duke, or a lord, or something of that sort, and he became quite enamored of the burnt-cork artists. Haverly lost money in London on his second trip abroad, but he expected to recoup on his tour through the provinces. He needed a stake to get out of the metropolis, so he talked his aristocratic acquaintance into making him a loan of £500, and gave him as security a mortgage on the show. Well, as it turned out, the troupe did make considerable money in the provinces, and when they were about to start for home the aristocrat ran down to Liverpool to foreclose his mortgage, not having heard from the Colonel as he expected. Jack gave him one of those famous sweet talks of his, and the troupe finally sailed for America, leaving with the Briton, in lieu of his hard cash, the first-part chair-covers and the bass-drum. It is safe to say that he will take no more mortgages on shows."

*<br>* *

"I had a letter to-day from Dan Maguinness, the old-time comedian of the Boston Theater Company," put in the Manager, as he tried to relieve his catarrh by loading the atmosphere with the fumes of a cubeb cigarette. "I was in the company with Dan years ago, when he first started in the business. He then used to load us up with the story that his salary was $75 per week. Every Tuesday we called at the box-office and were given our

envelopes.   Dan used to be on hand regularly, of course,
and he would hastily tear his envelope open, run over the
bills, tuck them into his vest-pocket, and then throw the
envelope away.   He always protested that he received
$75, but we hardly believed it.   Well, he came around
one day when the 'ghost walked,' and he went through
his usual motions, excepting that he tucked the crumpled
envelope into his vest-pocket, threw his salary away, and
walked off.   We saw it, and as soon as he turned the
corner we jumped for it.   When he hurried back, a few
moments later, pale and agitated, to look for his lost roll,
it was nowhere to be found, and of course none of us
had seen it.   The next day he advertised in the *Boston
Herald*, 'Lost—forty dollars,' and he never boasted of
his salary after that.   We returned his money, and he
hushed us up with a portion of it."

*<br>* *

The Proprietor, who had been up before the cigar-
case, "counting the house," walked majestically back to the
end of the bar and turned off the solitary gas-jet which
had been shedding its feeble effulgence over the group
since the midnight closing hour.   " You fellows will have
to knock off now," he said; and they knocked off and
filed out into the deserted streets, while the Purveyor
figured up the "tabs."

The last regular meeting of the Turnover Club was not held in the Usual Resort, but was called to order out on the hotel piazza at Cheltenham Beach, a resort after- ward named Cheataman Beach by Will McConnell— an appropriate name, in view of subsequent events. All of the members were present excepting the Purveyor, who was compelled to remain "on watch" in the Usual Resort, to slake the thirst of customers. In his absence, the hotel barkeeper was elected Purveyor *pro tem.*, and he acquitted himself admirably. The Manager had opened his heart and his purse, and proposed that the members seek a relief for the torrid heat somewhere on the cool lake shore. His kind invitation was accepted with great alacrity and unanimity, and through the kind- ness of a gentlemanly Illinois Central engineer, the party was safely landed at the beach. The first thing they did was to go out on the pier and load their respective lungs full of lake breeze.

\*<br>\* \*

"This is really glorious," remarked the Agent; "re- minds me so much of dear old Coney Island. Hope the beer is better here, though. At Coney they have stained- glass beer-mugs with elongated bottoms, and the quantity of really and truly beer they hold wouldn't extinguish a match. This beer is much better. I like to sit here and sip it, my heated brow fanned by the cool breezes from the lake. Reminds me of that pretty little 'Ode to Beer' written here in Chicago by George Arnold. He was a brilliant and well-known New York bohemian, and the story goes that he was here on a visit. He became 'flat broke' (a not uncommon circumstance with him), and while sipping a glass of beer and puffing at a donated cigar, one afternoon, in the basement at the corner of Washington and State streets, he took a bit of wrapping-paper which was lying upon the table, and dashed off the few stanzas. He tried to use them as a 'pot-boiler' and sell them to a daily paper here, but the poetry market was dull. The poem was subsequently printed in a New York paper, and prominent literary critics pronounce it one of the finest bits in the language. It runs like this:

> "Here
> With my beer
> I sit,
> While golden moments flit;
> Alas !
> They pass
> Unheeded by,
> And,
> As they fly,
> I,
> Being dry,
> Sit idly sipping here
> My beer.

> "Oh, finer far
> Than fame or riches are
> The graceful smoke-wreaths of this free cigar.
> Why
> Should I

Weep, wail, or sigh?
What if luck has passed me by?
What if my hopes are dead—
My pleasures fled?
Have I not still
My fill
Of right good cheer—
Cigars and beer?

" Go, whining youth!
Forsooth!
Go, weep and wail,
Sigh, and grow pale!
Weave melancholy rhymes
On the old times,
Whose joys like shadowy ghosts appear,
But leave me to my beer.
Gold is dross—
Love is loss—
So, if I gulp my sorrows down
And see them drown
In foamy draughts of old nut-brown,
Then do I wear the crown
Without the cross."

\* \*
\*

" That's a very pretty thing," commented the Actor.
" I'll think of that whenever I'm in hard luck. A glass
of good beer is a great comforter when a man is hustling
through a long summer without friends or money. It's
different when you are drawing a salary and can drink
wine. I tell you Ella Wheeler Wilcox had a great head
if she really did write that 'Laugh, and the World
Laughs With You' poem. I took a shy at that idea
myself the other day, and though I'm not much of a
poet, I'll take chances, with your kind permission, and
reel off the effort for you. If the Wheeler-Joyce combination brings suit against me, you'll have to back me
up. Here goes:

" Flush, and the crowd drinks with you;
  Broke, and you drink alone,
Provided, of course, you can borrow a dime,
  Or a barkeeper you can ' bone.'
Win, and your friends all join you;
  Lose, you are known nowhere;
A wallet full has a greater pull
  Than a pocket-book filled with air.

" Buy, and all men will love you !
  Pawn, and they turn and flee;
They're after your money, as fly is for honey,
  But your poverty they can't see.
Ride, and you pay the car fare;
  Walk, and they all roll by.
They are quick to hear if you sing out ' Beer !'
  But never do they call ' Zwei !'

" Lunch, and you settle the treat;
  If you're hungry, they never invite;
Earn and spend, and keep up your end,
  But few men will treat you right.
There is room in the gorgeous bar-room
  For liquor and cracked ice;
But one by one we must all sneak home
  If we haven't got the price."

* *
*

"Speaking of parodies," remarked the Agent, after
the applause had subsided, as he blew the white-caps
from off the surface of his glass schooner, "reminds
me of the time the Actor played *Orlando* in 'As You
Like It,' with Kelly's Shakesperian Megatherians.
There was a fellow named Percy Fitzmaurice, who used
to go on for *Jacques*, and he often did a parody on
the ' Seven Ages' speech in place of the original. It
went much better in the 'one-night stands,' too. I
believe he called it the 'Seven Stages of the Lush !'
I'll give it to you if you like." And there was a unani-

mous demand for it, possibly because it was thought that another round of applause would produce another rewarding round of applause, the Actor having responded to plaudits in that pleasing way. So the Agent arose and delivered, in a very fifty-dollar-per-week declamation, the following:

> "All the world will drink,
> And all the men and boys will help it out;
> They have their favorite beverages and haunts,
> And one man in his time plays many bar-rooms,
> His habits being seven stages.
>                 At first the dudelet,
> Taking a dash of ginger in his lemonade;
> Then the older dude, with his small salary,
> Buying the beer, unwillingly, for friends;
>                 And then the quiet drinker,
> Hitting the bottle with no great effort,
> Excepting a slight raising of the eyebrow;
> Then a Board of Trade man, full of mixed drinks, and beery,
>     like his pard;
> Jealous of great drinkers, sudden and quick in quarrel,
> Seeking to pour eight barrels, if he can find his mouth;
> And then the Justice of the Peace,
> In fair, round belly, with Isaac Cook's lined,
> With bleary eyes, and breath all full of cloves,
> Full of gin fizz and modern whisky sours;
> And so he plays his engagement.
> The sixth age shifts into the lean and bloated bum,
> With bunions on nose and thirst inside,
> His Sunday suit all torn, and his ulster pledged;
> And his noble voice as husky as green corn,
> Wheezing like the whistle of an asthmatic steamer.
> Last scene of all, that ends this strange, eventful tale
> In the inebriates' home, and mere oblivion,
> Sans wine, sans beer, sans credit, sans—everything."

*  *
*

"Bravo!" yelled the Manager, and the diplomatic applause which followed produced the wished-for result.

The Reporter had been a little uncertain about this, and
was making his beer last as long as possible; but when
he saw the dawn ahead he hastily gulped down what he
had left, and came up smiling for a third round.   When
he had secured his share of it, he volunteered to recite a
little poem about the old-time actor who saw nothing
good in the present, and was forever talking about the
"palmy days of the drama."   The poem, he said, was
entitled "The Old-Timer's Lament," and it ran like this :

> "The 'old-timer' sat on a dressing-room chair,
>     And lamented the drama's decay;
> He sagely spoke of those good old times
>     When he had had his day.
> He spoke of Burton, the elder Booth,
>     And sorrowfully shook his head,
> And said the drama was past and gone—
>     Then he borrowed a little red.

> "He spoke of his *Hamlet*, his *Macbeth*, and *Lear*—
>     How they differed from those of to-day;
> How press and public pronounced him peer
>     Of any who e'er held sway.
> Of the public he spoke; with sarcasm keen
>     Of the play we did that night;
> He declared that the drama was of the past—
>     Then he borrowed a little white.

> "'The young upstarts with more cheek than brains,'
>     Who ' pushed themselves to the fore,'
> Were mentioned by ' his old-times rocks,'
>     For they smote his heart's deep core.
> 'I'd like to see *them* in a round of parts;
>     They'd be lowered a peg or two.
> The drama now has gone to the dogs'—
>     Then he borrowed a little glue.

> "' The grease paints they use to make up the face
>     Were not used in the palmy days;
> A little burnt paper or white off the walls
>     Was enough for those good old plays.

No elaborate dressing, no furniture grand,
 Were needed to draw houses big;
Ah, the drama now is not as then !'
 And he borrowed the youngest man's wig.

"' The managers now are not actors as then;
 The big salaries that they pay
Are all a delusion, a myth and a snare—
 At least they don't come my way.
The leading man now has no fire or force—
 Act ? Why, who says he can ?'
With a sigh and a moan, and a face of his own,
 He goes on for a ' second old man.' "

    \* \*
     \*

"That's a good one," put in the Night Clerk, after the usual ceremonies, " and I have another little one on 'the perfesh' here myself. If you have ever had the misfortune to visit what is professionally termed a 'one-night stand,' you will certainly appreciate the force of the lines. Here goes :

"The 'one-night stand' on Michigan sand
 The hall-owner pictures with eloquence grand,
 And says that his is the best in the land,
  When he wants you to give him a ' date.'
 The ' public is hungry for just such a show,'
 The 'last one they had was two months ago,'
 And ' now folks are crazy to turn out and go,'
  So ' his locals' is prone to dilate.

"The day you appear the advance sale is light,
 But you're told it will surely ' pick up before night,'
 And, though 'the prospects don't look very bright,'
  You'll have ' all you can get in the hall.'
 This prophecy trite is true, strange to state,
 And, as the clock marks the hour of eight,
 You're told that ' the folks here always are late,'
  And sometimes they don't come at all.

"The music that's furnished makes singers feel blue—
 A cornet, a bass, a fiddle or two—

They laugh at the show, but they won't catch a 'cue,'
     And are always a little bit late.
Of course you can't kick, for they all have a trade—
Some work at the foundry, some handle the spade;
Strong, healthy men, yet of weak notes afraid,
     And they leave the 'comique' to his fate.

 '' The village hotel is not at all swell—
One towel, queer soap, no gas, no bell—
The eggs always out, the chicken as well,
     And breakfast is over at eight.
The landlord modestly asks 'two per day,'
And on the top floor stows 'the troupers' away,
And worries all night lest they will not pay,
     For 'shows have done badly of late.' ''

*  *
 *

"I have heard both of those last ones before, though
I do not think they have ever been published," put in
the Professor. "They were written by young Charlie
Warren, the comedian, who has a very keen sense of
humor.   Now I have one, of which I do not know who
the author is, though it sounds like Louis Harrison, the
comedian, who is great at clever jingles.   It is a parody
on 'The Yarn of the Nancy Bell,' one of W. S. Gilbert's
celebrated 'Bab Ballads,' and is called 'The Yarn of the
Manager Bold.'   It runs like this:

'' 'Twas near the town they call Detroit,
     In the State of Mich-i-gan,
That I met on the rocks, with a 'property-box,'
     A gloomy theatrical man.

'' His 'o. p.' heel was quite worn off,
     And weary and sad was he;
I saw this 'fake' give himself a shake,
     And he croaked in a guttural key,

'' Oh, I am the star, and the manager bold,
     And the leading and juvenile man,
And the comedy pet, and the pert soubrette,
     And the boss of the 'box-sheet plan.'

" He wiped his eye on a three-sheet bill
    ('Twas lettered in blue and red).
He cursed the fates and the open 'dates; '
    So I spoke to him, and said:

'' It's little I know of the mimic show,
    But if you will explain to me—
I'll eat my vest if I can digest
    How you can possibly be

'' At once a star, and a manager bold,
    And a leading and juvenile man,
And a comedy pet, and a pert soubrette,
    And the boss of the ' box-sheet plan.'

" He ran his hand through his dusty hair,
    And pulled down a brunette cuff,
And on the rocks, with his 'property-box,'
    He told me his story tough:

'' 'Twas in the year of '83,
    When a party of six and me
Went on the road with a show that's knowed
    As a musical com-i-dee.

" I writ it myself—it knocked 'em cold;
    It made 'em shriek and roar.
But we struck a reef and come to grief
    On the west of the Michigan shore.

" Each night it rained, or snowed, or blowed,
    And when the weather was clear,
They'd say, ' It's sad your house is bad,
    But wait till you come next year.'

" We traveled along from town to town,
    A tryin' to change our luck,
With nothin' to taste but bill-board paste
    And the 'property' canvas duck.

" At last we got to Kankakee,
    All travel-stained and sore;
But the star got mad and shook us bad,
    For a clerk in a dry-goods store.

" And then the leading heavy-man
 Informed me, with a frown,
He was going away the very next day
 With a circus then in town.

" The comedy pet and the pert soubrette
 Engaged as cook and waiter—
They are now doing well in a small hotel
 Near the Kankakee the-ay-ter.

" Then only the ' comic ' and me remained—
 For to leave *he* hadn't the heart;
Each laugh was a drop of blood to him,
 And he loved that comedy part.

" We played one night to a right good house—
 Eight dollars and a half;
But to my ill luck in my lines I stuck,
 And I queered the comedian's laugh.

" He fell down dead of a broken heart;
 The coroner, old and sage,
Said his brain was cracked with a bad attackt
 Of ' the center of the stage.'

" I played that piece all by myself
 For a week in Kankakee;
O'er rails and rocks, with this ' property-box,'
 I've walked to where I be.

" I never say an actor's good—
 I always damn a play—
I always croak, and a single joke
 I have, which is to say—

" That I am the star, and the manager bold,
 And the leading and juvenile man,
And the comedy pet, and the pert soubrette,
 And the boss of the ' box-sheet plan.' "

*  *
*

 " Say, boys," said the Agent, " I guess we have wor-
shiped enough at the shrine of the muse for one day,

and, besides, it's time for our train." And, as the sun slowly sank to rest in the western heavens, the members of the Turnover Club voted for adjournment, boarded an Illinois Central smoker, and started for the busy, teeming, bustling metropolis of the great lakes.

It was past midnight. The Usual Resort of the Turnover Club would have been shrouded in utter darkness
were it not for the rather feeble glimmer shed about by
the cigar-lighter at the end of the bar. At first glance
one would have declared the place deserted, but muttered
conversation from the vicinity of a table in the rear gave
evidence of life. Peering into the darkness, one might
have discerned the dim outlines of all the members
with the exception of the rugged contour of the Agent.
The Purveyor snored softly in a chair tilted back against
the huge ice-chest. His was not an aggressive snore,
but a plaintive, pleading, somnolent respiration, like
unto the bubbling of boiling mush. The Proprietor sat
in front of the table, his feet reposing on a neighboring
chair, and his eyes fastened upon the front door. He
spoke not, and the only sound heard was that of the
sibilant conversation going on between the Manager and
the Reporter. The Actor sat aloof, and occasionally
permitted the beverage in front of him to gurgle past
his collar. To the most casual observer it was evident
that there was a hen on, and that the Turnovers were
anxiously waiting its triumphant cackle. On the street
without, all was still. Suddenly, a blood-curdling shriek

rang out upon the clear night air and came ambling in through the open transom. It aroused the slumbering Purveyor, and brought the members to their various feet. It was the long-looked-for cackle. The missing Agent had arrived—but what was his condition? Again the silence was broken; this time by the lurid bric-a-brac of a drunken argument with an obdurate hackman. This battle of words waged fiercely for a few minutes, but it finally became evident to the watchers inside that some sort of a settlement had been arrived at, and they realized that the Agent had been out with his paint-pot, decorating the city with a rich vermillion tint.

The front door was tried, and then the latch was rattled vigorously. The Proprietor cast an appealing glance at the Purveyor, and that worthy went forward to admit the disturbance, who had begun a life-and-death struggle with a bar of "Sweet Violets." The key was turned, the door thrown open, and the Agent fell in with a dull, sickening thud. He was assisted to his feet, and led by the Purveyor into the presence of his disgraced fellows, every one of whom looked the gloom he felt shrouding his mind. With a trembling hand the Proprietor turned up the gas and revealed the form and condition of the fallen Agent. By a unanimous vote it was decided that he was a sight, and his pall-bearers carefully poised his person against the ice-chest, in order that he might not tip over and spill any of the liquor he had on board. In this position, he was soon wrapped in that deep slumber which knows an awakening through the agency of a large head—a head the size of which compels its unfortunate possessor, if standing on the main street, to walk a block away if he desires to scratch either side of it. In order to clinch the resolution that the Agent was a sight, the vote upon it was reconsidered and repassed.

A careful inspection of this "sleeper" who had been picked up, lent the impression that he had been dallying with a dynamite bomb. His vest was open, and the lower button of his plaid cutaway found a resting-place in its uppermost button-hole. One of his cuffs had climbed up on the outside of his coat-sleeve, and his necktie hung out over the back of his collar. The top of a vinegar cruet peeped out of his breeches-pocket, and the crown of his derby had entirely disappeared. A liberal portion of soft-shell crab rested upon his shirt front, and altogether he presented the miscellaneous aspect of an Irish stew. From one of his vest-pockets protruded the crumpled corner of a bit of paper, and the Manager ventured to secure this. It proved to be a pass from Chicago to New York. [NOTE.—This occurred before the passage of the Inter-State Commerce Bill.—*Author.*] The pass had been renewed so often during the progress of the Agent's protracted spree, that it resembled a Russian war map.

* * *

"According to what appears to be the last renewal of this pass," said the Manager, after a close inspection, " it expires to-morrow. It would hardly do, however, to put our unfortunate friend on a train in the morning. Besides, the pass is over the Baltimore & Ohio Railroad, and any man, even without such a head as the Agent will have when he wakes up, is liable to be seasick on that serpentine road. I remember once that I was traveling from Philadelphia, over that road, with Nat Goodwin and Ned Thorne, just after they had started out with their play, 'The Black Flag.' Thorne was very seasick, and when the conductor came through

the car in the morning, Ned grabbed the back of a seat
to keep his balance, and said: 'Say, conduc, I don't see
how you induce people to travel over this d——d crooked
road of yours.' The conductor, who had acquired his
sea-legs, smiled, and replied, 'People admire the grand
scenery along the line,' with a sweep of his hand toward
the panorama that was chasing itself around corners just
outside of the windows. 'Scenery be blowed,' was Ned's
rejoinder. 'Why, I've got a car-load of finer scenery
than that on this very train.'"

*
* *

"Louis Sharpe, of McVicker's, used to be John Stetson's stage-manager," put in the Actor. "He was with
him in Boston. One day Stetson came to the theater
and saw in front of the door an immense sign, reading,
'Grand matinee to-day at two o'clock, sharp!' When
John saw this he grew pale with anger, and rushed inside
to find Louis. When he discovered him, he dragged
him out to the sidewalk, pointed at the sign, and yelled:
'You d——d little cuss, I want you to distinctly understand that I am the manager of this theater! Now you
have that sign painted over, and make it read, 'Grand
matinee to-day at two o'clock, Stetson.' I played with
Stetson once, and the manager of our company told him
that the orchestra must be enlarged for our engagement.
Stetson said: 'This orchestra of mine is big enough
for anybody. I watched it last week, and I see that that
cuss in the corner with the drums don't play half the
time. If he'd only be made to attend to his work, the
orchestra would answer all purposes, and I intend to
read the riot act to him.'"

*
* *

"I met Charlie Reed, the comedian, to-day," remarked
the Proprietor, "and he told me a little fairy tale about

a little hunchback who officiates as janitor of the morgue out in San Francisco. The man's duty is to receive all dead bodies brought in there, and to care for them properly. For this work he receives a regular stipend, which is occasionally increased by a generous fee from some wealthy party, the body of whose friend or relative is found on one of the old man's marble slabs. One day a wealthy San Francisco Irishman turned up missing, and, after a long search, his two sons found the body at the morgue. They arranged for a swell funeral, for which the leading undertaker of the Coast provided an elaborate casket. This was taken to the morgue, and the hunchback, who had prepared the corpse for burial, lifted the body and carried it toward the coffin. As he did so, the lower jaw fell, and one of the sons cried out: 'Charlie, this can't be our father! The old gent had a good set of teeth, and these remains have none.' Charlie looked, and said, 'That's so, John;' and, after a close inspection, they concluded that it was not the body of their missing parent. They ordered the undertaker to remove the casket, and followed him out. The hunchback, who had confidently expected a particularly large fee, stood with the corpse in his arms and sadly watched their receding figures until the door closed behind them. Then he lifted the remains back to the marble slab, gazed pityingly at them, and said, in tones of deep reproach: 'You d—d fool! If you'd have kept your mouth shut, you'd have had a h—l of a fine funeral!'"

*_*_*

"I was talking to-day with a commercial friend of mine," said the Reporter, "and he told me about the experience of a Hebrew drummer who dropped in at his place the other day to show his samples. The young man was very pertinacious, and the first man he encountered was the proprietor of the store, who told him that his buyer was upstairs, and that they didn't care for anything in his line anyway. But the drummer insisted, and started upstairs to see the buyer, who was busily engaged with a customer. He saw the young drummer approaching, guessed his errand, and waved him off, but he opened his sample-case and started to expatiate upon the merits of his goods. Finally, he became so annoying that the exasperated buyer grabbed him by the collar, led him to the head of the stairs, and kicked him down. When he reached the first floor the proprietor saw him coming, and, divining what had happened, ran to meet him, and kicked him as far as the office. A salesman who happened to be passing at the time took a playful kick at the unfortunate Hebrew, and sent him as far as the door. Here the porter was standing, and he grabbed the young man by the collar and kicked him into the street. He fell into the gutter with a dull thud, but his business sense did not desert him for a moment. Picking himself up, he looked the store over admiringly, and ejaculated: ' Mein Got, vot a sysdem ! ' "

*
* *

"Say," blurted out the Purveyor, " I had a new game sprung on me the other night. I came out of Hooley's, after the show, and found a man at the entrance standing under an umbrella and selling duplicates of it for fifty cents each. The sidewalk was very wet, and, as I had a lady with me, I was obliged to part reluctantly with half a dollar. It was perfectly clear and pleasant when we went into the theater, and I was surprised at the sudden shower. We started off under the cheap umbrella, however, but when we reached the Sherman House I found the sidewalk dry, and, looking overhead, I saw the moon. That d—d umbrella peddler had watered the sidewalk

with a sprinkling-pot for half a block in front of the theater in order to dispose of his old stock.    It made me
sore to be bunkoed in that manner."

*·*

" Oh, our city is full of men looking after just such easy
marks as you," put in the Manager.    "But your speaking
of Hooley's, reminds me of the story Billy Crane, the
comedian, told me the other day, about how he and Robson came to surprise Nat Goodwin on the stage Monday
night.    Such a thought never entered their heads, he
said, until Louis James, late leading man with Lawrence
Barrett, proposed it.    He was sitting in their dressing-
room, and he asked how long a wait they had after the
second act.    When they told him twelve minutes, he
suggested the surprise to Nat, saying that they would
just about catch the carnival in the last act of the 'Skat-
ing Rink,' and would offend no proprieties by going.
Well, they consented, and James went over to look for
the opportunity.    After the two Dromios had responded
to the recalls at the close of the second act, they tied
their overcoats across their shoulders, jumped into the
carriage in waiting at the stage door, and were quickly
whirled over to Hooley's back entrance.    There they
found James awaiting them.    He cried, excitedly, 'Just
in time !  Nat's doing his imitations !  Rush !' and the
Dromios cast aside their overcoats, dashed down past the
veteran stage-door keeper; by the bewildered Cool White,
the stage-manager, who ran after them and vainly tried
to stop them; past the astonished actors, whose heads
popped out through dressing-room doors; they mounted
the stair-way three steps at a time, and were on the stage in
a twinkling.    Nat was giving his imitation of Barrett, and
had his back to them as they tripped on and threw their
arms around his neck.    Looking up into his startled face,

they both squeaked out, in Robson's treble, 'Welcome, dearest brother,' and Nat found voice for a characteristic ejaculation as they rushed off and down the stairs to their waiting carriage. They were driven rapidly back to the stage of the Grand, from which they had been absent exactly five minutes, and Joe Brooks, their manager, who entered their dressing-room a moment later, would not believe that they had been on Hooley's stage until both confessed to it. The thing could not have been worked better had it been planned for weeks beforehand."

\*\*\*

"John L. Sullivan is a great friend of Crane and Goodwin, you know," said the Professor. "He has been here during the week, and the other day he ran across Tommy Shea, who is Robson and Crane's business manager. 'Say, Tom,' he blurted out, 'where's Billy?' Mr. Shea replied that Mr. Crane was stopping at the Grand Pacific. 'Tus he know I'm in town?' asked the slugger, with an injured air. He knew the comedian well, and the fact that he had not hunted him up pained him deeply. He admires Crane and Goodwin very much, and in a party talking of professional people here, the other day, he said: 'Talkin' 'bout actors, t'ere's on'y two genelmen in de perfeshun. Dat's Billy Crane and Nat Goodwin—all de rest is duffs;' and his verdict was accepted without a murmur."

\*\*\*

"Your reference awhile ago to John Stetson," remarked the Proprietor, "reminded me that I saw him during my recent trip East. He showed me a very fine lithograph of Salvini, the tragedian, hanging in the private office of his Boston Theater. In one corner of the frame surrounding it was a printed card bearing Salvini's name. I pronounced the lithograph a fine piece of work, which it really was, and asked John if that was Salvini's autograph in the corner. He appeared perplexed, and did not answer. In a moment he turned and asked, 'What did you say?' I replied, 'I asked if that was Salvini's autograph in the corner.' He looked rather blank for a minute, and then said: 'To tell you the truth, I'm d—d if I know.' I have often thought that all these stories on John Stetson are rather far-fetched. There is one, however, that I can bet on. He was remodeling his theater at the time I was there, and he called me in to ask my opinion of the changes he was making. I carefully inspected the altered interior of the theater, and then told him I thought that the acoustic properties had been destroyed. 'The deuce they have,' he replied, indignantly. 'If anyone has destroyed those properties, then it's that blasted property-man of mine!'"

\* \*
\*

"Supper is now ready in the dining-car!" cried the Purveyor, as he threw open both lids of the nickel cracker and cheese casket and pushed the dish of olives toward the members. Some time was spent in a discussion of the viands, and the worn-out Agent was deposited in the ice-chest, after which the Purveyor turned off the gas, made a record of the state of the meter, and closed up.

# IV.

When the gavel fell at last night's meeting of the Turnover Club, the Agent removed a large piece of tobacco from the midst of his back teeth, and remarked that he had been a martyr to toothache during the week. " Last Monday," he said, " I was in here, partaking of one of the Purveyor's celebrated clam-chowders, and I accidentally ran across one of his macadam clams.  It caught two of my back teeth amidships, and caved in the rear elevations, allowing a small-sized nugget to fall out, leaving two exceedingly sharp edges behind.  After these had made several unique scroll-saw designs upon the inside of my cheeks, I dropped into a drug-store and invested in a piece of spruce gum.  After chewing this awhile, I inserted the gob in the new cavity, with an exalted idea of my own cunning.  But it absolutely refused to harden worth a cent, and, after I had allowed it to play ' peek-a-boo' with my tongue for about an hour or so, I sought a dentist, who removed the gum, sawed off the serrated edges, and afforded me temporary relief. The next day I had the discrepancy carefully examined by the man who originally filled the molars.  He first surrounded it with a rubber blanket, which he appropriately called a ' dam,' and then prodded the cavity in his

search for the nerve. Well, he found it; and it is a singular coincidence that I found it at the same time. I
never knew before that the nerve of a man's tooth had
any connection with his shoes, but I found that such was
the case. After he found it, he covered it up with a little
'rough on nerves,' and then told me, after he had jammed
it down securely, to return when the nerve was dead. I
will do so; but I imagine from present sensations that
the nerve is still in the heart of the city."

\*\*\*

" I was chatting with a manager of 'the good old days,'
the other afternoon," said the Actor, "and during the
course of the conversation he asked me if I had ever ran
across a player who could render *Hamlet's* part correctly,
without a mistake. When I told him that I thought
Edwin Booth was letter-perfect in the role, he gave me a
most surprising bit of information. He said that Forrest
was the only actor who ever knew the lines of the part
perfectly, and he once asked a friend how many mistakes
he thought Booth would make in the part. The friend
said he did not think he would make any, and the manager offered to wager him a bottle of wine on every five
mistakes as long as he cared to accept the wager. The
bet was made accordingly, and soon afterward Booth's
old prompter joined the party. The question was referred
to him for his opinion, and he ventured a guess of two
hundred mistakes. This the manager's friend refused to
believe, and he asked the old prompter if he had ever
'held the book' on Booth. He replied that he had done
so in *Hamlet* over four hundred times. That night
Booth played *Hamlet*, and the manager's friend 'held
the book' on him himself—that is, he did so until he
had noted one hundred and thirty mistakes, when he
went outside to 'see a man.'"

"I met young Charlie Frohman here the other day," put in the Manager. "He is just back from a protracted Western trip, and tells many good stories. While up on the line of the Northern Pacific Road he met a party of players who were billed heavily as the 'New York Lyceum Company No. 1.' When Charlie asked one of them if his brother Gus was with the company, the man had the nerve to say that he was. The troupe was announced to play 'Fanchon,' 'Hazel Kirke,' 'Hamlet,' 'Uncle Tom's Cabin,' and other little skits of the same caliber. They had been playing along the road from town to town, to $10 and $15 houses, spending a week in each small place. The 'leading man' left every Friday night to 'bill' the next town, and the 'property-man' played his part Saturdays. As this leading man was manager of the company, and was engaged to the leading lady, he had things pretty easy as far as salaries went. One day they struck a town where a convention was being held, and at night they had a packed house, taking in more money than they had seen during the entire season. After paying all expenses, the manager found himself the happy possessor of $149 in bills and silver, and the next morning he called his people together in the hotel, and said: 'Ladies and gentlemen, it's a cool, bracing morning—now for a dash to the depot.' They dashed, and the acute manager saved eight 'bus-fares thereby. When they reached the station, the manager asked for the ticket-agent, and when that worthy appeared at his window, in response to the summons, the disciple of Thespis shunted his $149 through the aperture, and said: 'Please give me eight tickets at theatrical rates.' The ticket-man asked where to. 'East,' said the manager. 'Just figure up how far east that will take eight of us.' The bewildered agent scribbled

away, and finally remarked: 'That money will buy eight
tickets from here to Winona, Minn., and leave $1.15
over.' The manager ordered the tickets, then turned to
his people, and said: 'Ladies and gentlemen, we go to
Winona, Minn. I will have just enough left to wire my
agent that I do not need him any longer.' Then the
party gathered up its 'props,' appearing glad of a
chance to escape from the fastnesses of the Wild West."

\* \*
\*

"Their agent?" added the Manager, as someone
asked what became of that individual. "Well, he got
left, as Charlie said. The manager himself was usually
his own agent, but on this occasion he had sent the
property-man ahead, that there might be one less hotel-
bill to wrangle over. Frohman met the unfortunate man
in a town some miles farther up the road. It was about
dusk, and it was bitter cold. Charlie was hurrying along
toward the hotel from the telegraph office, wrapped in a
heavy ulster, when the deserted agent halted him, and
shook his hand with the lofty air of a prince of the blood.
He wore a long linen duster, white plug hat, and his low-
cut shoes and pants were wide apart. Frohman's teeth
chattered with the extreme cold as he charitably invited
his new-found friend into the hotel, where it was warm.
But his invitation was refused by the bankrupt agent,
who urged him to go out and see the town. The poor
fellow had not seen a quarter in weeks. 'Fine, bracing
weather for this time of the year; eh, Charlie?' he said,
as he tried hard to look comfortable. He had just
learned of the troupe's cruel desertion of him, but he had
no regrets to express; and there he was, all alone and
apparently happy in his misery, with no baggage excepting a box of Den Thompson's lithographs which the
manager had sneaked out of some theater where they

played. The deserted agent declared his intention of going ahead and billing Den Thompson with the 'Lyceum Company,' and charging his board-bills back on the company, until the lithographs gave out. Then it would be time to think of doing something else."

*
* *

"Were you fellows in here the other night when Nat Goodwin, the comedian, threw John L. Sullivan, the pugilist, out into the street?" queried the Agent. " No? Then I'll venture to tell you about it, as it was very funny. There was a large party of professionals here, indulging in the flowing bowl, and John L. was the center of an admiring group who were feeling of his arms and pinching his biceps. Nat, who is one ot his particular friends, came in quietly, took off his coat in the little room there, and borrowed an immense Colt revolver from the Proprietor. Sticking the 'gun' in his pistol-pocket, he walked up to Sullivan, tapped him on the shoulder, and said, in an angry tone: 'See here! you've given me trouble enough, and I want you to clear out of my place.' The strangers at the bar pricked up their ears, and one or two of the more cautious sneaked out via the side door. 'Go on, now,' continued Nat; 'you're a big, bean-eating coward, and I've had enough of you. Go on!' The big slugger had 'dropped' to Nat's little game, and he attempted to apologize; but the comedian was obdurate, and he finally took Sullivan by the collar and pulled him toward the door, while the strangers stared in wonder, and began to whisper, 'Who is he?' Nat kicked the slugger and pushed him at the same time. He fell upon the floor, scrambled to his feet, and rushed into the street, while Nat swaggered back and handed the gun to the barkeeper. Sullivan slid around to the side door, stuck his head in, and said, meekly: 'Please, mister, I'd like to come in ; I won't raise a row.'   Nat looked at him a moment, appeared to ponder, and then replied: 'You can come in again if you'll buy a bottle of wine, and behave yourself; but if you make any further disturbance, I'll knock the whole top of your head off.'   John bought the bottle, and the strangers sneaked up to Nat to feel of his arms and legs on the quiet."

*
* *

"Many's the time 'on the road' that I would have given a dollar for a piece of pie like this," said the Manager.   He had been hitting the lunch-counter, and as he separated his face from a rim of pie, he continued: "When I was ahead of Colonel Boozby's 'Triple Uncle Tom Company,' I was riding, one day, on a train between Burlington and Peoria, when the conductor happened to inquire the name of my company.   After he had passed along, a 'jay' who had overheard the question and answer, turned to me and said: 'You theayter troupe people must have darned good times !'   Well, I had been awakened a few hours before by a '5.30 call,' and I said 'Yes,' with a very large smile.   One night during the following week we played until 11 P. M., caught a train at 2.12 A. M., rode until 5.43 A. M., fretted in a country station for two long hours, and then caught another train and rode until 12.30 P. M.   The next morning we were obliged to arise at six o'clock, after playing at night, and, to keep us in training, we had a 'three A. M. call,' a three-hour wait, and a late arriving hour for dessert.   And still there are people who think that we 'theayter troupe people have a darned good time.'   I remained with that show until Colonel Boozby wanted to cast me for one of the bloodhounds, and then I quit.   The next summer I played in a 'snap' stock company in a small town.   The

'jays' continued to make me very weary, and the popu-
lace of twelve hundred souls united in giving me a cramp
in the scarf-pin. One fine evening I was strolling along the
street toward the theater, and I overheard one of a knot
of Reubens standing on a corner say: 'These play
actors will have a goll darned nice night for their ting
tung.' Then they asked in that town if we 'carried our
own screens' with us, and told us that we 'acted right
well up on the stagings.' I was captain of the local ball-
team during that summer, and one night I was cast for
*Bob Brierly*, in the 'Ticket of Leave Man.' It was so
frightfully hot that I didn't use any make-up, and went
on with a smooth face. The next afternoon, an aged
'jay' came up to me on the ball-field, and said: 'I knew
you on the stage boards last night even if you did wear
whiskers, b'gosh.' Fine encouragement for a man with
talent, wasn't it?"

\* \*
\*

" I ran across John Russell the other day," remarked
the Counsellor. " He, you know, is a great friend of
John Stetson—used to work for him. When Russell was
in New York, recently, he dropped in at the Fifth Avenue
Theater to see the 'Mikado.' The house was packed.
Between the acts he met Stetson outside, and said:
'Nice business, isn't it, John?' Stetson confessed that
it was, in his opinion. 'If I were you, I'd drive the speculators away from the doors, though,' remarked Russell.
'How in thunder can I do that?' queried Stetson, testily,
flaring up at once. 'I tell you what I will do, though,'
he added. 'They've got their licenses, but if this court
decision is made in their favor, I'll raise the price of seats
to $2. D—n it, I'll protect the public!' 'But,' remon-
strated Russell, 'they'll raise to $2.50.' 'Then *I'll* make
it $2.50,' said Stetson. 'There's no limit to my game.'

**4**

While they were standing there, up came four of Stetson's friends whom he had invited to see the show. He had forgotten all about the invitation, and there was not a box or a seat left; so he was obliged to apply to the hated speculators. These gentry are all down on him; and when he took four seats and asked the price, the man said: 'Twelve dollars, please.' 'What's that!' yelled Stetson. The speculator named his price again, and, after gazing at him from head to foot for a moment, he said, throwing back his coat: 'Here, I've got three or four hundred about me—just go through me!'"

*<sub>*</sub>*

"Our friend George Ryer was here the other day," chirped the Reporter. "You know he traveled once with Herrmann, the magician, whom he can imitate to perfection in voice and manner. He used to guy the wizard to his face, but Herrmann never 'tumbled.' It was a part of George's duty to provide the necessary material for all of Herrmann's tricks. For one trick he had to procure two cheap silk hats, one of which he gave to the magician and the other to a confederate whom he planted in a certain seat near the stage. Herrmann knew this seat, and always approached its occupant when ready for the trick. One night, this seat was sold by mistake, and George put the confederate as near as possible to it, though he did not care much whether Herrmann found him or not. Well, when the wizard came forward to borrow a silk hat, he of course made for the regular seat, and the gentleman who had bought it, and who occupied it, proffered his own expensive silk tile. Herrmann supposed it was the confederate's hat, so on his way to the stage he fell on it, crushing it, and then kicked a hole in it and playfully tore off the brim. This ruin done, he jammed the remains into a mortar and shot them

skyward.  Then a brand-new silk hat fell to the stage, and
Herrmann picked it up, brushed it gracefully with his
silk handkerchief, and politely returned it to the man,
who tried to put it on.  It was a cheap hat, about
two sizes too small for the owner of the destroyed
tile ; and when the wizard saw his mistake, he gnashed his
teeth and rushed from the stage.  The next night, the
confederate who disappears in a cabinet and appears
mysteriously in the parquette circle was arrested by
a green policeman, who caught him rushing through the
alley from the stage, thinking he was a thief ; and Herrmann waited in vain for the *denouement* of his trick.
He was not in good humor that week, as you can
imagine.  Everything turned out all right, however."

*<br>*

"Speaking of turning out," said the Proprietor,
"reminds me that it is time to turn out the gas ; "
which he proceeded to do, while the Purveyor turned out
the Turnovers.

# V.

The regular weekly meeting of the Turnover Club was held last evening, in the Usual Resort. By arriving at an early hour on the ground, the Reporter secured the floor; and when the gavel fell, he was in full possession. The solemn, six-beer look upon his face indicated that he had something of grave import to communicate. After clearing his throat in the manner peculiar to the Club members, he said he had a very momentous proposition to make. Of course they all liked to hear fairy-tales and aged "walnuts" about theater folk, and these usually formed the chief topic of their gatherings; but he thought it was high time for them to ascend to a higher plane, and discuss the all-absorbing questions of the hour. To test the sense of the meeting, he would move that at the next session they take up, for general debate, the topic: "When the telegraph wires are all put under ground, what will become of the men with spurs on their boots, who now earn their livelihood by climbing the telegraph poles?" This, the Reporter maintained, was a question touching the welfare of many happy homes; then he paused for a reply. The Manager said that they were all with him on the "higher plane" idea, but he thought the stride proposed was too great for a starter.

If they decided to become literary guys, they should get there by degrees. They were not by any means a Browning Club, and were weak on many points in literature and history. Indeed, the Agent had gone so far at the previous meeting as to declare that "Romeo and Juliet" had been written by Pedro Gonzales, or some other man with such a cigar-box name. If they decided to start up after this higher plane, they should start in modestly, with a curriculum not so far above their heads. They might begin by discussing the vital "lithograph question," or "how an agent can buy wine on $30 per week," or some such elementary topic, which was a part and parcel of their every-day lives. "Let the pole-climbers dig in their spurs," he said, "and shift for themselves;" and with one great, unanimous accord, the Club sat down upon the Reporter and his elevating proposition.

\* \*
\*

"Heard of John Russell's new scheme yet?" queried the Agent, as he reached over and filched an olive when the Purveyor's back was turned. "He has discovered a new and attractive method of naming chorus people on the programmes, and he says it will be adopted by all of the comic opera companies on the road next season. His idea is to name the chorus-girls after towns, and the chorus-men after well-known points of interest. Here is one of his schedules for a 'Mikado' chorus;" and the Agent carefully unfolded a piece of paper and read as follows: "'Japanese maidens—Lulu Boston, Millie Poughkeepsie, Marie Marshalltown, Sadie Oskaloosa, Tillie Toledo, Katie Keokuk, Pauline Pullman, Madge Milwaukee, Ann Arbor, Minnie Apolis, and Sarah Cuse; Japanese voters—William Niagara, Charles Obelisk, Henry Bartholdi, Brooklyn Brydge, J. Bunker Hill, Yellow S. Park, Y. O. Semite, Horse S. Bend, Cliff

House, and Hell Gate.'" "You see," said the Agent, "the general public never cares to read the names of the chorus people on their programmes; but if John's plan is adopted, every comic opera cast will be a complete geography lesson in itself. The scheme could be worked like patent-inside newspapers, and, as John says himself, it's 'a corker.' Just think of its possibilities!"

\* \*
\*

"If I had my way," remarked the Actor, "I'd have the death-watch stationed outside the cell occupied by that German dumb-waiter of yours," addressing the Proprietor. The Actor was evidently in a very bad humor. There were deep, dark lines of care under his eyes and upon the visible edges of his collars and cuffs. When questioned as to the particular nature of the Teutonic Ganymede's alleged crime, he said: "Why, the chump has no more sense than a three-sheet poster in two colors. I came in here yesterday afternoon with my entire week's washing, for which I had just paid an almond-eyed 'washee man' thirty-four cents. At the time, I was in a joyous mood, and when a friend invited me up to drink, it was in this same gay spirit that I handed my immaculate linen to that libel on Germany, and told him to put the bundle 'on the ice' until I called for it. When I called for it, last night, the blue-ribbon idiot fished the bundle out of the ice-box, where a lot of lobsters and soft-shelled crabs had been having fun with it. The collars and cuffs looked exceedingly dejected. You should teach your foreign hirelings the English language before you spring them upon an unsuspecting public. Now," addressing the Purveyor, "if I asked you to put a round of drinks 'on the ice' for me, you'd know what I meant, wouldn't you?" The Purveyor said he would, but he would not do it, all the same. "That's all right,"

said the Actor; "but you'd not put the drinks where a
refrigerator full of soft-shell crabs and lobsters could
get full on 'em.   Here I am with no clean collar and
with soiled cuffs.   Why don't I reverse the cuffs?   I have
—and you knew it, too.   There was no need of your
calling attention to the fact, either.   Wrote a topical
verse on one of them last night for young George Boni-
face, the comic opera comedian.   He wanted a verse on
the fat stock show for 'Read the Answer in the Stars,'
and I wrote him a corker about reading the answer in
the steers.   It so pleased the stockmen, they sent word
to George that if he would come down they would kill
a fatted calf for him ; but he refused, politely.   He has
been in the comic opera business too long not to know
of what material the average fatted calf is composed.
You can't throw any sawdust in his eyes !"

\* \*
\*

"This tooth of mine is bothering me again," complained the Manager.   "Is there anything worse than a
toothache?   I remember once that poor John McCullough, the tragedian, had a raging toothache during a
performance of 'Virginius' here.   The tooth started in
to howl vigorously while he was engaged in 'making up'
for the part, and he had no time to seek a dentist.
During the entire first act he was in great agony, and he
ordered his stage manager to send out for a dentist
at any cost.   But dentists are hard to find at that hour,
and McCullough's tooth was playing the 'Star-Spangled
Banner,' with variations.   In the market-place scene,
he had a chance to relieve himself somewhat; and
the way he did denounce *Appius Claudius* was a caution.
Ned Collier played the part.   After that act, the dentist
came into the dressing-room and examined the refractory
molar.   Like all of his profession, he wanted to save and

fill it ; but McCullough cried, ' Out with it ! ' It was a pretty sturdy tooth, and the tragedian hung to the straps of his wardrobe trunk while the dentist yanked. It finally came, and the operation left poor John in a somewhat wilted condition. He didn't have to ' make up ' much for grief in the last act."

* * *

" George Primrose, the minstrel man, was saying, the other day," put in the Night Clerk, "that he used to live in London, Canada, and I heard him tell Billy Crane, the comedian, that he used to wait on him at the Tecumseh House there very often. That was long before Crane was known to fame—while he was stealing through the provinces over the border with the Holman Opera Company. It was a sort of a family company, and one of the sons was idolized by the rest as its comedian. Crane used to sit in the wings every night and watch him play—worshiping him from a distance. Finally, this flower of the family died, and there was great sorrow in the camp in consequence. No one could be found to play his comedy parts, and at last Crane volunteered to try them. Of course he was laughed at; but after a time they consented to have him take a flyer at the rôles. They told him he could take the parts and study them, but he said he already knew them, through witnessing his predecessor's performances. Well, he made a big hit. He tells me that while with that company he played *Devilshoof, Uncle Tom, Don Cæsar*, and the clown in a pantomime, all in one evening. For all of this he received thanks, for they gave him nothing else excepting his board. One happy day, Mrs. Holman gave him a ten-dollar bill, whereupon he rushed to the express office and sent it home, fearing to carry that much money about him. Now he lights cigars with twenties, they tell me."

"Frank Daniels, the comedian, is just back from San Francisco," said the Counsellor; "and he told me that while there he ran across a smart tramp, named Rivers, who used to be in 'de perfesh,' and who is now out on the Coast in that uncertain condition popularly known as 'broke.' Rivers is an eccentric individual, who goes about with play-bills on his arm and sprigs of celery stuck in his coat-pocket. One night he raised a row in the parquette of a variety theater, and a burly policeman started to drag him out. 'Hold on!' he cried, 'I want to say something;' but the policeman was obdurate. Finally, however, the officer consented to allow Rivers to have his say. His old professional training came back to him, and pointing his finger at the leader of the orchestra, he yelled: 'Hey, cull, give me a "hurry" in G.' The leader obligingly gave the chord, and the policeman gracefully hustled Rivers out in that key."

*.*

"Ever hear of a 'nickel-shooter'?" queried the Agent. "It's a new one on me, and I only heard of it the other night. These tramps who hang around the West Side cheap lodging-houses occasionally run across a nickel, which they invariably invest in whisky. In the 'barrel-houses,' which they patronize, they get a large glass of so-called 'liquor' for five cents, and if they don't drink it all, the residue is poured back into the barrel. Well, this mode of procedure broke the hearts of the tramps, and they finally devised the 'nickel-shooter' idea. A man would swallow all he could of his drink, and then hold the remainder in his mouth. When he got outside, he would take his partner aside and inject the dose of fire-water down his gullet as a mother bird would feed her young. That's what is called a 'nickel shooter,' and they tell me the operation can be witnessed almost every night near these West Madison street barrel-houses. It's too far along for us, though."

\* \*
\*

"When Frank McKee was billing Charlie Hoyt's 'Tin Soldier' company in St. Louis, last week," said the Agent, "he tried to work up an advertising dodge anent the two bogus soldiers in the play; so he spent two days in looking after one-legged tramps. He could not find one in the town ; so he engaged two of the most disreputable looking soldiers of fortune he could find, took them to the theater, and assisted nature a very little by reddening their noses, blackening their eyes, and making their personal appearance twice as tough. Then he rigged one leg of each on stumps, dressed them in soldier's clothes, and armed each with an old musket. As a final precaution, he gave each one of them three dollars, and directed them to start out and buy a glass of beer in every saloon in St. Louis. This portion of their contract they filled — also themselves. At night, McKee lost them, and feared that they might have got drunk and pawned their regimentals ; but a detective found them slumbering in a disreputable saloon, and res- cued the trappings of war. McKee gave up that scheme, and the next day he asked permission of the depot- master to put a lithograph on the face of his clock. He was refused the privilege. Then he resorted to Ben Stern's idea of advertising for two thousand cats and setting them adrift with advertisements of his show tied around their necks. He is a hustler."

\* \*
\*

Just here the Agent was interrupted by a terrible fit of coughing. The Purveyor said he had been trying to cure him of eating all of the cheese on the lunch-counter by substituting neatly cut bits of soap for the genuine article.　He thought he had succeeded, as the Agent was frothing at the mouth.　The Agent made a wild dash for the Purveyor, but the Proprietor separated them, and declared a hasty adjournment.

# VI.

When the Turnover Club members turned up in the
Usual Resort last evening, the Purveyor was in no cheerful mood. His name was wolf, and it was his right to
howl. As he erased with his towel the foot-prints of
three beers from the mahogany before him, he glowered
savagely upon the Agent, who cowered in terror behind
the cracker-and-cheese receptacle. He declared that he
was in extremely hard luck. He always did hate Febru-
ary, he said, because his salary was $25 per week, and
there were but four weeks in the month. Besides, everything had gone wrong with him—burglars had entered
his lodgings, chloroformed him, and then robbed him.
When he awoke from his stupor and found what had
happened, he discovered his pants out in the hall, his
coat in the front yard, and his vest up on the roof.
Everything had been taken—even his photograph—and
all the midnight marauders had left him was a bottle of
cough-syrup, a box of corn-plasters, and an odor of
chloroform. It was indeed a sad tale, and as the Purveyor related it, he wept with one eye, and kept the other
securely fastened upon the crackers and cheese in the
Agent's vicinity.

"I was told, the other day," put in the Actor, "about a chowder club which used to meet down in a little Massachusetts town. It was composed of a lot of old-timers, who gathered every year at a clam-bake, and indulged in a glorious time. One day, one of the oldest members of the club up and died. His widow made all of the funeral arrangements herself, and she fixed the ceremonies for the day of the annual clam-bake. Of course, this would never do, and the club appointed a committee of one old tough to wait upon the widow. He did so at the earliest possible moment, and he told her that 'the boys' desired very much to attend the funeral of their dear friend, but that they had ordered their clams for that day, and were afraid they might spoil. He asked, on behalf of the club, that the obsequies be postponed at least one day. But the sorrowing widow declared such a thing impossible, as all of the relations had been invited. She feared, too, that the remains might spoil if kept longer. 'Where are they?' asked 'the committee,' as he shifted his quid. 'In the parlor,' replied the widow; and 'the committee' went in and inspected them carefully. As he sadly turned away, he looked at the widow and said, in a reassuring tone : 'Sweet as a nut; keep for a week!' And the clams were saved."

\* \*
\*

"Hear that one on our old friends St. Peter and St. Paul?" queried the Agent. "No? Well, it's a good one. It is related of them that they were shaking dice upon a certain occasion, and that St. Peter shook five sixes in one flop out of the box. Then St. Paul rattled the 'boot-leg,' and spilled out five sevens. This was too much for St. Peter. Disgust curled his upper lip, and he said, scornfully: 'Hold on, there, Paul—no miracles between friends.' At this interesting point," continued the Agent, "the festivities were interrupted by a loud rapping at the pearly gates, and St. Peter quit the game to go and see who was there. It was a Chicago man who was seeking admission, and St. Peter accorded him a discouraging bluff by slamming the gates in his face, without saying a word, just as soon as he learned where the applicant hailed from. 'That's all right!' shouted the Chicago man. 'I'll get dead even with you!' And he went away over in a further corner of the yard, clapped his knees vigorously with both hands, and loudly crowed three times. St. Peter opened the gate on a crack in a moment, beckoned cautiously to the Chicago rooster, and when he came up, St. Peter said: 'That'll be all right, partner; let by-gones be by-gones.' And the visitor from the champion summer resort bowed himself in."

\*\*\*

"I ran across John Doris, the circus man, the other day," remarked the Manager. "He told me he had just returned from a trip through Mississippi with his show; and he said he hoped never to go down there again. Saw a man shot or cut nearly every day, he declared. John's brother, who is a ministerial-looking chap, did the heavy oratory for the side-show, and John told me of a very funny experience he had down there. It was the custom to help out the side-show by giving some free exhibition outside of the canvas, for the benefit of the natives; and the usual attraction was 'Professor Etherio, the flying man,' who did a rope-walking act. This treat was announced during the progress of the usual street parade, and usually a large crowd visited the vicinity of the tent. After the 'Professor' had done his flying, Doris' eloquent and clerical-looking brother took the assemblage in hand, and told the usual fairy tales about the 'curiosities, monstrosities, and freaks of nature' to be seen on the inside. He always wound up his talk with something like this: 'Now be careful that you purchase a ticket for each member of your family; and be sure that you read these tickets carefully, without asking any questions. The price of admission is but a dime—ten cents—and one ticket admits you to all parts of our great world's fair. You still have a full hour before the performance begins in the large pavilion.' One day, in a certain Mississippi town, the regular programme had been carried out about this far, the crowd being composed of about eight hundred people, mostly colored, when a tough-looking citizen, standing a few feet in front of the lecturer, started suddenly, whipped out a wicked-looking six-shooter, and opened fire on another party, quite as tough looking, who was standing in the crowd, about twenty feet away. As he fired his first shot, he yelled: 'You —— —— —— ——, I've been looking for you for six weeks, and, —— you, I've found you at last!' It appeared afterward that they were brothers-in-law, and had vowed vengeance upon one another at sight, on account of some family row. The man who was made a target, pulled his ever-ready gun, and proceeded to return his assailant's fire. Some half-dozen shots were fired back and forth, but no one was hurt. It scared the crowd, though, and in about two minutes Doris saw the interested gathering and its hard cash melt away like the snow in April. And now he will not even pass through the State."

*<br>* *

"Speaking of circus men," put in the Manager, "reminds me that I met 'Jumbo' Davis here the other day. He is the man who purchased 'Jumbo' for Barnum and brought him to this country. We were walking along Clark street together, and we met a bright-looking colored boy, who was nattily attired in a plaid suit. He stopped to chat with Davis a few minutes, and in answer to a question as to how he was getting along, he said: 'I don' tink I'll haf to eat snow-balls dis winter, sah!' When we left him, Davis turned to me and remarked: 'That coon is a great character, and is one of the very best "Zulus" on the road. He was born in Erie, Penn., and has traveled as a "Zulu" with circuses for many years. You'd never know him if you'd see him in his "Zulu" rig. He has a heavy ring in his nose, big rings in his ears, and wears a woolly wig. Then he wears only a scant breech-clout, and carries a spear. Pretty cool for him late in the season, but, bless you, he don't care; and he can talk more "Zulu" than you ever heard. Sells his photographs, too, and makes big money. The only favor he asks is to be allowed to lay off when the show he travels with is in Erie. He is afraid some of his old playfellows there will give him away. It is a safe bet to back his statement that he will not be obliged to eat snow-balls next winter, for he's not that kind of an American Zulu.'"

*
* *

"Our friend Billy Crane, the comedian, experienced rather an unfortunate week before he reached here," said the Counsellor. "In Wheeling, he left a valuable silk umbrella in his dressing-room at the theater, and when he went to recover it, early the next morning, he was almost told that he was a liar, and had not left it there. The next day, he received a telegram from New York announcing the untimely demise of the pretty little Yorkshire terrier he had purchased for Mrs. Crane. The animal was run over by a hansom cab, on Broadway. It cost Mr. Crane $50, and its 'necessary expenses' have

5

been as much more, so there was a loss of a cool hundred. Then, in Dayton, he was sitting in his dressing-room, when a member of his company came in to borrow his mirror. On the lower edge of this mirror rested the comedian's beautiful diamond ring, for which he paid $475, and it rolled off the mirror-frame in the hall-way. As its loss was not discovered until after the performance, it was never recovered. There was a net loss of about $600 in one week; but this loss was off-set, however, by the prize which awaited the comedian here. It was the photograph of a beautiful society lady, who wants to go on the stage, accompanied by a note stating her wish. As Mr. Crane does love to put beautiful society ladies on the stage, he is happy—though he is most always happy when free from dyspepsia."

\* \*
\*

"The best cure for dyspepsia that I know of," declared the Night Clerk, "is plenty of exercise. Long walks are sure to cure a man of it. Actors are greatly troubled with indigestion, because of their late hours and late suppers. But Harry Meredith, the actor, never suffers from dyspepsia. Why? Well, because, in traveling between small towns, he often walks, thereby getting plenty of exercise, and gladdening the heart of a manager by saving one railroad fare. I remember that when he was starring in 'Ranch 10' he scared his manager, Slater Smith, nearly to death with one of his freaks. Slater had been up very late one night, celebrating that most unusual thing in dramatic circles, a good house in a 'one-night stand,' and he went to bed exceedingly tired. About one A. M., he was awakened by a rustling sound in his room, and raising himself upon one elbow in bed, he glanced toward the door. There he saw on

the floor a writhing, snake-like object of white, and without further ado, he sunk back on his pillow and covered
his head with the bed-clothing, quaking with fear the
while, and wondering if 'they' were in his possession.
The next morning he arose, after a series of fitful slum-
bers, and, with an effort, glanced toward the door again.
There he saw upon the floor the long, white margin of a
newspaper page. It appeared that Meredith had decided, at a late hour the night before, to walk on to the
next 'stand' (a distance of fifteen miles), under the
beautiful, moon-lit sky, and being utterly unable to
arouse his manager, he had written his intentions upon
the strip of paper mentioned, and by degrees slipped it
under his door. When the company reached the next
town, they found Meredith seated upon the hotel piazza,
calmly enjoying his morning cigar, and greatly refreshed
by his nocturnal jaunt. That's the way to stave off dyspepsia. Other actors are obliged to walk, anyway; but
then, they don't have enough to eat to receive the dyspepsia."

* *
*

"I have noticed something during the past week that
has pained me exceedingly," said the Reporter. "I
allude to the pictures of Colonel Haverly which have
been adorning our windows and dead-walls. In the
olden times, these works of art were brighter and more
cheery; now, they appear dull and colorless by contrast.
Why, I remember the day when, in these counterfeit
presentments of the king of minstrelsy, Colonel Haverly
wore a blue coat, a red vest, and a purple necktie. More-
over, he was represented pictorially as possessing green
eyes, pink cheeks, orange hair, and an ecru mustache—
seven colors in all, I believe, besides a tint. Has there
been a recent rise in colored inks, or are the present ones

the old lithographs with the colors faded out? Alas,
poor Haverly!"

\*\*\*

"You know, I suppose, that both Tom Keene, the tragedian, and Harold Fosberg were among the actors who
fought for the Union?" put in the Professor. "Well
they were, and Keene often used to spout in camp for his
fellows in blue. On a certain occasion, a big benefit for
the Sanitary Commission was given in the Grand Opera
House, in New York City. The play was 'Hamlet,' and
the star was the noted Count Johannes. The immense
house was packed from pit to dome with a well-disposed
audience; but after the Count had masticated a few of
the melancholy Dane's speeches, the people began to
guy him unmercifully. Keene was cast for *Laertes*, and
when he made his first entrance the audience started to
have fun with him. This, though, was too much for Tom.
Forgetting all about 'Hamlet' and *Laertes*, he strode
down to the foot-lights, shook his fist savagely at the
great gathering, and yelled: 'I want you people to understand that I am just from the front, by God!' 'Hooray!'
yelled the delighted audience. 'I've fought for your
country, and now I'm here to do what I can for my sick
comrades!' 'Hooray!' was the roar, as *Hamlet* sneaked
off the stage, and Tom Keene began to writhe and twist
as he does now when he recites the 'Star-Spangled
Banner.' As a benediction, he yelled: 'I don't propose to be insulted in doing it, either!' 'Hooray!'
shrieked the thoroughly captivated audience; and the
performance of 'Hamlet' was then resumed at the point
where the thread was broken off. Every time Tom
Keene came on the stage, the great audience yelled
'Hooray!'"

"Come, come, gents," interrupted the Purveyor at this point, "it's time to close up.  I'll just give you a hard-boiled egg each, in honor of the glad Easter morn which has just arrived;" and the members stood up in line, silently partook of the solidified "hen-fruit," employing condiments to the taste, after which they adjourned for one week.

# VII.

The atmosphere surrounding the meeting of the Turn-over Club in the Usual Resort last evening was decidedly pugilistic. It had been thoroughly impregnated by the presence in the city during the week of the most noted sluggers of our own fair land, together with fistic contributions from England and Ireland. The Club's conversation throughout the evening was densely interspersed with playful badinage and sparkling repartee, which involved such unique phrases as " knocking out," and " hitting on the kisser," and " putting to sleep." Several famous prize-ring contests which live in the history of the squared circle were fought over again, through the eloquent medium of the mouth, and the Agent arose upon his ear, and threatened to " put a head " on the Purveyor if that valued member did not cease the disagreeable practice of serving him with popped beer. The king of the prize-ring, Mr. John Longfellow Sullivan, of Boston, had been a guest of the Club, as had Mr. John Sautvoord Dempsey, of New York, and Mr. Charles Tennyson Mitchell, of London, England, all of whom had indulged in promiscuous oral glove-fights " to a finish " beneath the admiring ears of the Agent's friends. Business in the Usual Resort had picked up so amazingly under the patronage of this muscular galaxy that the Proprietor had been obliged to secure for the Purveyor an "understudy," whose duty it was to fill bottles and wash glasses during the few interims. Altogether it had been a very large week, and the members looked it—especially the Agent. "I see," he remarked, "that John T. Raymond, the comedian, has been playing at Hooley's during the week. Joe Whiting is in the company, and a short time ago they were in an eastern theater where electric lights are used. At a matinee performance during the engagement, some of the younger members of the company attached one of the electric wires to a chair which Joe was to occupy in the next act. Before he came onto the stage, the wire parted by accident, but as Frank Lane made his entrance in the first scene, he stooped and adjusted it again. In a few moments, Whiting came into the entrance and looked onto the stage. Mr. Raymond had been let into the secret, and he and Lane groaned inwardly, as they thought Joe had discovered their trick. But he had not, and when he came on he sank into the chair and began to talk. Suddenly, in the very middle of a sentence, he bowed himself up, with a frightful whoop. The audience saw the point, and howled with merriment. It soon came Raymond's turn to sit in the same chair, but before he did so he was careful to kick the wire away. He is an odd genius, that Raymond. I wonder if he is still as fond of matching as ever? Guess he is, for it's a habit that's hard to break. I remember well when he matched poor Sam Medill for a column advertisement in the *Tribune*—and won it, too. Raymond asked Sam to write the advertisement for him, and he agreed to do it. In the middle of the column was the comedian's

advertisement proper, and the rest of the column
was filled up with: 'Match him!' and 'Match him
if you can!' in type of all sizes. It created a great
deal of talk at the time, and the uninitiated wondered
at it."

*<sub>*</sub>*

"I had a man in here the other day," put in the Proprietor, "and he was a daisy. He asked me if I could get
him a nice lobster, and I had him served with a beauty.
To demonstrate to him that I had really done well by him,
I proceeded to expatiate upon the beauties of the bird,
when he interrupted me by saying: 'You can't tell me
anything about shell-fish, and particularly lobsters. Why,
I was born and raised where they come from! I have
often gone down to the beach, which was within a short
distance of where I lived, and have fairly seen the water
on fire with lobsters!'" The Manager was obliged to take
all of the members aside and explain this story by telling
them that when lobsters were in their native brine they
were green, not red, and the water could not very well
appear to be on fire with green lobsters. This diagram
plainly showed the shot, and all laughed excepting the
Actor, who attempted to defend the man who had called
for the lobsters by saying that there was such a thing as
green fire—he had seen some of it touched off once
when he played one of the witches in the tragedy of
" Macbeth."

*<sub>*</sub>*

" Frank Lane, of Raymond's Company, told me a good
one, the other day, on our friend ' Jumbo' Davis," said
the Agent. " The incident happened to him once when
he was with a circus. One day the show struck a small
town, and Davis hired the local brass-band to lend éclat and
noise to the parade, promising the musicians two dollars

each for the éclat, and each a free ticket to the show for
the noise.

"Well, the band did bravely, apparently caring more for
the free ticket than the two dollars, as they created more
noise than éclat.   However, when they were paid off, a
number of them went to the village store and spent their
money for éclat, and just before the afternoon performance began in the large pavilion, two of the musicians
turned up at the main entrance.   Both were very full.
When they winked knowingly and attempted to walk in,
they were halted by Davis, who demanded their tickets.
They explained that they belonged to the local brass-
band.   'Jumbo' said he knew that, but he had given the
musicians all tickets.   At this, the fuller of the two
men said he had lost his ticket.   'Oh, that's all nonsense
—you couldn't lose your ticket,' said Davis, then thoroughly indignant, because he thought they had given
away their tickets.   The spokesman for the pair straight-
ened himself up and replied, with an effort, 'The h—l we
couldn't lose our tickets! I lost a bass-drum!'   And
Davis passed them in."

* * *

"After scaring us for a week with his processions of
armed men upon our streets in these troublous times,"
remarked the Manager, "Jim Herne has produced his
new play, 'The Minute-Men,' at the Grand.   Herne is
an old-timer, by the way.   He used to travel around the
country as a manager some years ago, and he ran some
pretty queer shows.   I remember one season he had a
lot of gorgeous printing, setting forth an extensive repertoire, and he traveled with six people.   They did not
carry a stitch of scenery, and Herne's plan was to rely
solely on his showy printing to fill the houses.   After the
money was all in, he would go before the curtain and say:

'Ladies and gentlemen—I am here to offer an apology, and I wish to be fair with my patrons. The fact is that, through some annoying error, our car-load of scenery has gone on to the next town, and consequently we are without it. Now we propose to ask your indulgence under the circumstances, but if there are any present who feel so disposed, they can have their money refunded at the box office.' Of course, these remarks always met with a generous round of encouraging applause, and no one went out. After this the six people proceeded to give a very lame performance of 'Hamlet,' without scenery or costumes, and the audience had no chance to kick. Since those days Herne has 'caught on.'"

* *
*

"I heard a good one, the other day, on Charlie Hoyt, the author of 'A Rag Baby,'" put in the Professor. "When traveling, he always carries with him a board, a hammer, nails, and a lot of foolscap paper. These articles he has in his room at the hotel where he stops, and when he is lying in bed at night he thinks of a good many new and clever points for his farce comedies. When one of these novel ideas strikes him, he jumps from his bed, seizes pencil and foolscap paper, and hurriedly jots it down. Then he takes the board and nails the idea to the floor, in order that it may not escape him. In the morning he releases the happy thought and dresses it up. Why, there is one room in the Palmer House which he always occupies, and the carpet is just full of these nail-holes. I have been told that one night 'Hoochy-Coochy' Rice, the minstrel man—they always call Billy 'Hoochy-Coochy,' because he invariably says that whenever he comes on the stage—entered Hoyt's room with a dark lantern and a jimmy and stole a new song which the author had just written and nailed to the

bedstead.   I hardly believe this, though, as I have heard
Billy Rice very often, and never knew of his having anything new."

\*\*
\*

"Speaking of Hoyt," said the Reporter, "reminds me
of the big boom John Russell gave his latest play, 'A
Tin Soldier,' at the New York opening.   It was a great
piece of booming, I can tell you.   You know that the
Excise Law in New York City is very strictly enforced,
and at certain hours the bars are covered by huge
muslin shades, upon each of which is a sign reading,
'Bar Closed.'   Taking this as a suggestion, Russell procured hundreds of neatly printed signs, bearing the
legend, 'Bar Closed, by Order of A Tin Soldier,' and
these were hung up on the muslin shades all around
town after hours.   He also procured similar signs for
the barber-shops, which all close at a certain time.   Then
he secured space on tall buildings opposite each of the
city theaters, and hung up huge advertisements of the
play.   At night these were illuminated by the brilliant
electric lights of the theaters over the way, and all
theater-goers were forced to see them.   The crowning
stroke, however, was his work at the first League base-
ball game, on the Polo grounds.   About twelve thousand
people were present, listening to the music, and wishing
the players would hurry onto the field.   It was an hour
before the time of calling game.   Something happened,
and twenty-four thousand eyes were riveted upon three
men, clad in overalls and carrying paste-buckets and
ladders.   They appeared in the outfield, walked toward
the lower fence, and there began to paste bills.   A great
big 'A' went up first, and the crowd wondered what was
coming.   Then the whole—'A Tin Soldier'—went up
in sections as the crowd gazed at the fence, and then a

shout went up for the ingenuity of the advertiser. It was great booming all around, and the result was that the play turned people away from the unluckiest theater in New York for weeks."

\*\*\*

"James O'Connor Roche, the author of Kate For-sythe's new play, ' Marcelle,' has done a good deal of the entertaining this week," said the Night Clerk. "He told us a good one about a tramp who ventured into a New York bar-room, last fall, in quest of alms. It was a raw and chilly night—Thanksgiving eve—and the tramp was lame and poorly clad. To employ Mr. Roche's classic language, ' he had kidneys in his feet;' hence his faltering gait. But he was a veritable ' Chesterfield in rags ' withal. Leaning against the highly polished bar were a group of actors, ' in for reorganization.' The tramp politely lifted what remained of his hat, and said: ' Gentlemen, could I ask you for a dime, wherewith to procure food and a night's lodging?' There was a gen-eral shaking of heads among the actors. ' You may have a turkey concealed about your person,' continued the outcast. ' To-morrow is Thanksgiving, and I have little to be thankful for.' At this appeal the cold hearts of the histrions melted, and the pennies that were forth-coming were received with regal politeness and profuse thanks. A spirit of guying seized the group, and as the poor tramp faltered toward the door, one of them asked, ' What is the matter with your feet, my friend?' Half-turning, he answered, ' I stepped on a lighted cigar, sir,' and then he resumed his weary way. ' Where are you living now?' was the next question shot at him from the group. ' Hush,' whispered the tramp, mys-teriously, ' I'm not living at all—this is only a bluff;' and he was gone."

"Roche tells another good one, at the expense of the West Division Railway Company," said the Counsellor. "He jumped on the front platform of a street-car down town, one cold night last winter, to ride over to the Academy and see his play, 'Shane-na-Lawn,' in which Billy Scanlan is starring. It was not too cold for his necessary smoke, and he braved the blast for the sake of his weed. The driver, a stumpy little Irishman, slapped his breast and stamped his feet in a vain endeavor to keep warm. 'Cold night, my friend,' volunteered Roche. 'Indade it is, sor,' came in a rich brogue from beneath the heavy muffler. 'Been long with the company?' was Roche's next query. 'About twilve year, sor—kim up, there!' to the horses. 'You must be quite a favorite with the company, then,' came from between the puffs of Roche's cigar. 'That I am, sor. D'ye say that ould gray mare there, an the nigh side? Well, lasht summer her an' I wor tuk sick at the sem toime. The cump'ny sint fer a docther fer her, an' docked me. Oh, yis, Oi'm a great fav'rit wid the cump'ny, Oi am, sor;' and Roche jumped off at Halsted street."

\*\*\*

Just here the Proprietor noticed that several members of the Club limped painfully when they walked, and he was informed that they had been inveigled by alleged friends into playing a game of base-ball, a few days before, in nines captained respectively by Sullivan, the slugger, and Muldoon, the wrestler. Five innings had been played when the game was called "on account of mud." It had been great sport until the next day, when aching joints and bruised fingers had their innings, and then the members were actually "dead sore." Each one bore marks of the ball as it had come from the ample hand of Mr. Sullivan, and in bathing-dress they would have readily passed for tattooed men. Besides this, they had been assessed one dollar each to defray the burial expenses of the umpire, who had been the unwilling victim of a strike, and a third strike at that. And so the members sat around and nursed their bruises with a lotion compounded by the Purveyor, looking as though they would willingly issue a challenge to Fox's martyrs to martyr against time for the gate-money. They sat there until they heard Sullivan at the front door, asking if there was any truth in the report that certain members of the Club had been talking about him. If so, he was anxious to find the man. In a minute, the Club hastily adjourned through the rear door in a body.

# VIII.

When the Turnover Club met in the Usual Resort last evening, the Agent and the Actor were busily engaged in perfecting the details of a scheme which both agreed would inflict at least partial paralysis upon the Nation. It was the creation of the Agent's fertile brain, and its very audacity astounded the members. His idea was to establish on a prominent thoroughfare of the city a "spectacular lunch-room." The Stoddard lectures had always been so popular that he saw no reason why a restaurant conducted upon a similar plan would not make an instantaneous and decided hit. The rooms would be darkened during the phantom meals, by heavy curtains, and colored views of the various courses would be thrown upon a large sheet by a powerful stereopticon, while the Actor would lecture from the stage upon each dish as it was shown. Fumes from the nearest restaurant would be brought in through pipes, in order to complete the illusion. In this way, by charging a very small admission fee, a man could partake of a course dinner without fear of the pangs of indigestion which attend the actual hearty meal. It would commend itself particularly to actors "resting" for the summer, as "the profession" would always be recognized at the door. Artists were now employed, the Agent said, in taking photo-

6

graphs of various dishes served at Mr. Kinsley's food
emporium, and already a most life-like picture of a ver-
mouth cocktail had been secured.   This would be
exhibited prior to each exhibition meal, as an appetizer.
As each course appeared upon the sheet, the lecturer
would pause until each one in the room had seasoned it
to his taste, when the proper fume would be turned on
and the lecturer proceed.   A counterfeit presentment
of a good table claret would be served in an annex, at a
slight advance.   Course tickets would be on sale at the
leading music-stores, and there would be an entire change
of bill every week, to accommodate the holders of these
illusory meal-tickets.   It was unanimously agreed on
all sides that this idea of the Agent was entitled to position in the bright lexicon of the Club as a synonym for
the word "corker," and the members all promised to
attend the exhibition of the opening meal.   All that the
Agent feared, he said, was that the constant attendance
of the Actor as lecturer would dangerously overload his
stomach.

*_*_*

"I have noticed during the past week," put in the
Manager, after the excitement had subsided somewhat,
"that the 'dizzy actor' is reaching the town in great numbers.   I see many of him down on Clark street here every
day.   His wardrobe is usually very light—not enough of it
left to make an ample and satisfactory pair of pantaloons
for an able-bodied man.   He wears paper cuffs, and
every morning he carefully scissors off the soiled edges,
pulls them out of his coat-sleeves a little further, and
then readjusts the safety-pins.   He laundries his own
collar with an erasing-rubber and a hunk of billiard
chalk.   How he lives, no one can tell.   He could take a
pair of these paper cuffs and a two-dollar bill and go

around the world without changing either. Yet he
appears to have all the beer he wants, and to be cheerful
withal. Verily, I say that the 'fakir' is a mystery no
one can successfully solve."

* *<br>*

" Jim Roche told me another good one the other day,"
remarked the Counsellor. "About two summers ago he
accepted an invitation from Ned Thorne, the actor, to
visit him at his summer home near Long Branch. When
he arrived there, he found Ned and his brother William
busily engaged in moving into the house a lot of furniture
that had just arrived. William was attired in a pair of
long overalls tied over his shoulders with bits of rope, and
both were working hard. Of course, Roche, even though
a guest, started in to help them, whereupon Ned stopped
lifting and merely laid his hands on things, saying he was
afraid he might break them. Mrs. Thorne remonstrated
with him for allowing their ' company ' to labor, but he
declared that he could not prevent him from so doing if
he insisted. The job was finally completed, however,
and that evening the three men drove over to Long
Branch. While sitting in the reading-room of the Ocean
House—Ned's favorite resort—a Jerseyman entered
with a lot of woodcock and some eels. Thinking that
this combination would make a great breakfast, Ned
purchased a mess and took them home, where they
were placed in the ice-box over night. This ice-box was
outside of the house, and when William arose, bright and
early the next morning, he found, to his dismay, that
some enterprising tramp had entirely cleaned out the
larder. Ned was informed, and when he learned the
true state of affairs, he awoke half of the Branch with his
forceful comments. William suggested that they should
have a watch-dog, and then Ned remembered that

McKee Rankin had once promised him a fine one, so he telegraphed him to ship the animal at once by express. Two days later the household was seated on an upper balcony, when the front gate was opened by one of two Jerseymen who carried between them a huge box. The Jerseymen were pale but calm. Dropping the box in the center of the gravel path, one of them walked up to the door, thrust out a book to Mrs. Thorne, and said, 'Sign,' in a very husky voice. The package was receipted for, and the Jerseymen hastily took their departure. Then the household ventured out to examine the box and its contents. One side of the box was slatted, and through the slats peered the bloodshot eyes of a young mastiff, who appeared to own a head as big as a court-house and teeth like rows of Washington monuments. 'Nice doggy,' crooned Ned, rather doubtfully, as he surveyed his prize and snapped his fingers from a respectful distance. The response was a fearful growl, which fairly crunched the gravel beneath the box. 'Let him out, Bill,' said Ned, as he reached the top step. 'Not with these overalls on,' responded William; and the household retreated and gazed at the box from the balcony. Pretty soon a big Jerseyman who did chores about the place came into the yard, accompanied by his small yellow dog. This intrusion was too much for the mastiff in the box. With a howl of rage, he bounded through the slats, and the Jerseyman and his dog disappeared over the fence in a great hurry. The mastiff owned the place, and he at once proceeded to promenade around the house without interference. Everyone who went along the road after that was saluted by Ned with a yell of, 'Hey, come and kill a mad dog!' but no one accepted the invitation. Finally, along came a Jerseyman who said he would go and get his gun, and as he plodded off up the road, the two Thornes and Roche whistled ' Johnny, Get Your Gun.'  In ten minutes, he returned with it over his shoulder, and entered the yard. At first he did not see the mastiff, but the mastiff saw him at once and made a wild rush for him.  With a frightened cry, the fellow dropped his gun and cleared the high fence with a bound.  Then, Mrs. Thorne settled matters by quietly going down to the front door, calling the dog, patting him affectionately, and becoming his friend at once.  She started to lead him upstairs, when Ned and William rushed into their respective chambers, locked themselves in, and threw the keys out of their windows. Roche, being a guest, did not run, though he felt mighty nervous, he said, as the huge animal walked up and carefully inspected him.  The dog began to feel at home then, and thereafter he was as gentle as a lamb; but Roche says that was one of the most exciting days he ever put in, and he has seen great excitement."

*  *
*

"Have you heard about the menagerie of William Ananias McConnell?" queried the Agent.  "Well, you know he had a rooster up near his flat, and the bird murdered sleep in a frightful manner; used to hold conversations at early dawn with a cousin who scratches gravel in Pullman.  A sign in the hall-way of the flat building read, ' Please leave calls with rooster; ' that was when a tenant wanted to arise early.  One very dark night, Will arose, captured the disagreeable boy chicken, and took him to the pound, where he pounded his head off.  All went well thereafter until the bereaved family in the lower flat purchased a female goat to replace the dead rooster. Recently, Will has been adorning the interior walls of his barn with lithographs of ' show people,' and, on the evening of the day the new goat arrived, he started for the barn to tack up a lithograph of 'Dr. Jekyll and Mr. Hyde.' The goat ambled after him. As there are eleven clothes-lines stretched across the yard, and as Willie has no burning desire to cut his throat, he has to crawl to the barn, which is at the end of the lot. When he had tacked up the lithograph, he started to return to the house, but the goat was awaiting him, and there was fire in his eye, so Will went out through the alley and sought the front door. Last Monday, he lost four shirts, and did not know what had become of them until he saw the goat expectorating shirt-buttons. Now he uses a large scantling when he goes to the barn, and declares that he will brain the animal if she molests him."

\* \*
\*

" This Pauline Hall, of the ' Erminie ' company, has a novel admirer in the person of a Chinese dude from Harvard," said the Actor. "When the company was in Boston, recently, this Celestial witnessed the performance, and was so deeply smitten with the fair Pauline that he at once sat down and indited a letter in his native language. She showed it to Francis Wilson, the comedian, and he pronounced it a wash bill, advising her to pay it and avoid trouble. Then she showed it to Charlie Parsloe and John Ince, the stage Chinamen, and they translated it for her. She learned that the Chinese student had written her Chinese words of burning love, with the end of a tooth-brush, on brown wrapping-paper, and she was supremely happy at the conquest. Since that time, the Chinaman has attended nearly every performance of the company, and he threatens to follow her here to Chicago. Some of the local Sunday-school students have heard of their swell countryman's intentions, and will lay for him when he arrives and do him up at bung loo."

"The air was blue up around the artists' studios last Thursday afternoon," said the Professor. "The bluish tinge emanated from the studio of Gean Smith, the well-known horse painter. Now, you are quite well aware that Gean has a big reputation as a delineator of fiery steeds—in fact, when a man sees one of his race-track scenes he at once looks around for a bookmaker's stand. Well, last Thursday, a man dropped in on him and approached him in a most mysterious manner—a Herr Most mysterious manner, in truth. 'Are you the horse painter?' he whispered; and Gean said he was. 'Then I've got a great scheme,' the individual went on, in a hoarse whisper. Visions of a great big order floated around the atelier. 'I've got a big mare,' buzzed the visitor, 'and if you can paint her, I think we can "ring her off" at some of the Southern meetings this winter. I think you'd better paint her brown, be '—but Gean hustled the man out to the elevator shaft and dropped him into the well beneath. Then the blue air floated out lazily through the studio window as the artist expressed his opinion of the fellow."

*<br>* *

"I heard the other day of an experience that George Middleton, the museum man, had once in Australia," put in the Reporter. "You know, of course, that all Australians are very loyal to Queen Victoria. Well, George went over there with Cooper & Bailey's circus, and was anxious to make a big hit. Among his attractions was a big hand-organ, with which he expected to capture the natives. After the show had been in the country some days, he was advised by an Australian to have some popular airs put in the organ; so he sent for new barrels, and when they arrived he put them in, one night, and looked for a big sensation. About 8.30 P. M., he gave the organist the signal, and that worthy proceeded to grind out 'God Save the Queen.' The effect was magical, but unlooked for. The entire audience arose as one man and deliberately walked out of the tent, in spite of Bailey's yells that the show was not over. The following night, no one came to the tent, and Middleton asked the hotel proprietor what the trouble was. 'Your show is too short,' he said. 'The people don't get their money's worth.' And it was only then George learned that in all shows in that country the tune 'God Save the Queen' is regarded by the audience as we regard 'Home, Sweet Home'—as a signal for dispersing. So George shifted that tune to the last act, and did well thereafter."

\* \*
\*

"I see," broke in the Manager, "that the Reporter has ignited and is engaged in smoking another piece of rope. That is usually the signal for adjournment;" and the members faded away for a week.

When the members of the Turnover Club met in the Usual Resort last evening, the Reporter appeared with his neck swathed in bandages, and the Agent was desirous of knowing if he had gone into training as a rival of Barney Baldwin, the man with the dime museum broken neck. "No," was the scribe's response; "I wear these samples of dress-goods around my neck for the reason that the other day my person was separated from a small but vigorous wen on the o. p. side of the epiglottis. Owing to its awkward location, I was unable to make it do service as a collar-button, so it had to go. When I applied for the separation, it looked as though there might be trouble; but when the surgeon's keen-edged knife entered an appearance, I imagined that something in the nature of a cross-bill must have been filed. However, the trial resulted in my favor; but I expect that when the surgeon files his bill for alimony I will be forced to schedule out. During the past week, I have had eighty-four men ask me what the matter was, and when I replied that I had had a wen amputated, eighty-three of the questioners asked 'When?' The eighty-fourth was a deaf mute friend of mine, whose

lead-pencil broke off short, fortunately, when he started
to spring the gag himself. A friend of mine in the
show-printing business is getting me up a lithograph
to give as a souvenir to the hundredth man who asks
me the question."

* * *

" I notice," remarked the Actor, " that they are playing Bartley Campbell's old piece, ' How Women Love,'
over at the Wonderland, and I want to show you how
men love. Here is a letter from an orchestra leader to a
lady in the company he was with at one time. I'll read
it just as it is written. Here goes: ' Dear Friend May
—Before commencing my letter I ask your pardon to let
you wait so long for a letter, but I have been bussy
arranging music last week. I was verry much disappointed not to find you at the depot wen I left to give
you the good-bye kiss—but I send you one whit this
letter. I give you two as soon as I see you again.
I guess you are still busy all day writing Contracts & ect.
We done fair business last week. I am verry lonely for
all the lady's in our company are married. I wish only
you were whit us. I suppose you are still eating your
little pie every morning—I am sorry that I can't help
you. You must excuse me but I think of you all
the time, your black eyes shine in to my heart most all
the time. They have captured my heart—it is gone, if I
would be surden of your love, it be some relief—I will
now close my letter by sending you thousands of kisses.
Yours to the end.' Well, I guess I'll not read his name,
and I would rather not divulge the name of the lady who
is in the habit of eating pie in the morning."

* * *

" This Inter-State Commerce Bill is playing havoc with
the cheap companies," said the Manager. " They are

having a hard time on the road, just now, to scrape up full railroad fares. The other day I ran across George Deyo, who has just arrived in town after a suc- cessful season with Scanlan, the Irish comedian, of 'Peek-a-boo' fame. George was telling me that some of the 'James Crow' managers were getting the best of the railroads by employing fewer people in their compa- nies, and making each man in their hire play many parts. A certain manager of this stamp hired an actor to play three separate and distinct parts in one play. It was a formidable task, but the salary was small and sure, so he agreed. One evening, the manager met him and handed him the three parts to study. The following morning the actor hunted up his employer, and returned him the parts, saying: 'I can not do this work—it's utterly im- possible.' 'And why not?' was the manager's surprised query. 'Because in the first act two of the parts quarrel and the third one separates them, and I'm blowed if I can see how I can play all three—I'm no Saxe-Meinmingar company!'"

*
*  *

"The young son of old Tony Denier, the pantomim- ist, had a great deal of fun last week," put in the Agent. "Among his numerous acquaintances is a Polish market- gardener, who has a hot-house out near Washington Park, and raises parsley and sich for the city trade. He professes to be a confirmed anarchist, and is always say- ing that he would delight in pitching an out-curve bomb at some bloated capitalist. Young Tony guys him, and tells him he is no true anarchist; that he is not a No. 6, and that he wouldn't throw a bomb if he had one. Such talk exasperates the Pole, and he protests vigorously that he would like to bathe in capitalistic gore. One day, early in the week, Tony took some friends out to this

fellow's place with him, and in his pocket he carried a
*papier-maché* stage-bomb of his own manufacture. The
party found the alleged disciple of Herr Most in his hot-
house, and the last man to enter, closed and locked the
door. In the course of the conversation which ensued,
the gardener's favorite subject was broached, and young
Tony began his usual tactics. Finally, he said : ' I don't
believe you would throw a bomb, and I am going to test
you.' He took from his pocket the pasteboard engine
of destruction, calmly lighted its fuse with his cigar, and
then bowled it down the middle alley of the hot-house.
In the mad rush for the door which followed, the blood-
thirsty anarchist went under the wire several lengths in
the lead; and when he discovered that the door was
locked, he presented a picture of abject terror, until the
paper bomb fell apart with a slight puff and a squirt of
smoke. Then he did get mad; and he threatens to get
even with young Tony, at the first opportunity, through
the medium of a real bomb—no *papier-maché* affair."

*<br>\* \*

" Let me tell you fellows it is fortunate that you are
not wearing the usual thirty-day badge of mourning
for a deceased member," remarked the Proprietor.
" The Counsellor had a narrow escape from a violent
death, at my hands, last Monday. He was celebrating
the Fourth of July, and he came in here in the evening
looking exceedingly innocent and child-like. But his
looks belied him. When I wasn't looking, he sneaked
down to the lunch-counter and cautiously inserted a
large common fire-cracker in the heating-oven. Lighting
it with his cigar, and then closing the door carefully, he
moved off to await developments. The developments
arrived on schedule time. It was an awful explosion,
and it distributed the contents of the oven in all direc-

tions.  An innocent customer who was sitting at a table near by, engaged in disposing of half a lobster, had his back hair combed and oiled with a plate of asparagus, and a sirloin medium shot out of a side door and fell in the alley with a dull, sickening thud.  Meals were strewn everywhere, and the frightened cook fell back upon the broiler, with the most painful results.  Something led me to suspect the Counsellor of the vile deed, and I made for him ; but he was too quick for me, and made good his escape.  I'm sorry now that I didn't kill him.  The very best I could do, under the circumstances, was to lump all of the distributed meals and adorn his 'tab' with the amount."

\*\*\*

"Speaking of common fire-crackers," put in the Agent, "reminds me that I saw a sensation created with one the other day.  A man who was pretty full entered a wet grocery where I was standing with a party, and while the purveyor there was mixing the drink he ordered, he sat one of those large red holocausts on the bar and touched off the strings with a cigar-lighter.  It had just begun to sizzle when we all discovered it.  The purveyor saw it at the same time and dropped to the floor with a yell, while we all rushed wildly for the door.  'Hold on!' yelled the stranger.  'Whatcher 'fraid of?' And he pinched out the sparks between his fingers, removed a pasteboard cap from the top of the cracker, and pulled out a roll of circulars, which he proceeded to distribute in the now curious crowd.  He was an agent for an accident insurance company which had adopted this novel method of advertising its business.  We all laughed at the joke, but the purveyor couldn't get over it.  He said it was mean to play such a trick on a man who had heart disease."

"When George Gore, the New York fielder, was here with his nine, last week, I asked him the meaning of the base-ball term 'charly horse,'" put in the Actor; "and he told me that little Joe Quest, the old Chicago player and umpire, had introduced the phrase into the League. By trade, he said Quest was a blacksmith; and when he was at work in a foundry, some years ago, it was quite a common occurrence for a man who swung a heavy hammer continually to be affected with a sprain of the muscles and tendons of the fore-arm. The workmen called this ailment a 'charly horse;' and when Quest introduced it into base-ball, it was at once adopted and given a broader meaning, and made to include sprains of all tendons and muscles. This is said by Gore to be the real derivation of the curious term."

\*\*\*

"Lou Weed, the fat and handsome treasurer of Aronson's 'Erminie' company, who now adorns the door of the Grand at every performance, is a great story-teller," remarked the Agent. "One day, while in New York, he was standing in front of the Casino, just before a matinee, with Will Daboll, of the company, and he called the latter's attention to a slender, finely built young man who was approaching, saying: 'There comes John L. Sullivan's trainer.' Daboll sized him up, and wanted to know if he could fight. 'I guess he can,' replied Lou. 'I saw him lick six big men on Sixth avenue one morning.' The trainer paused to chat, and was introduced to Daboll. When he started to leave, he offered to shake hands with Weed; but Lou knew him, and declined the grip. Not so Daboll. He reached forth his good right hand, and in a moment it was inclosed in a vise of iron and almost wrenched off. 'Hold on, there!' yelled Daboll. 'I've got to use that again;' and as the sport tripped laugh-

ingly up the street, the actor carefully examined his fingers and said, 'Yes, I guess he can fight.' "

*
* *

"That man Daboll greatly admires sport and sports-
men of all sorts," put in the Night Clerk. "He stops
down with us at the Tremont, and the other afternoon he
stood in the rotunda, gazing at the members of the
Detroit and St. Louis base-ball teams, who had just been
playing one of the world's championship games here.
After his eyes had drunk in the massive proportions of
each player, he strolled toward the elevator and took a
seat in the car. Following on his heels was big Dan
Brouthers, the giant first-baseman of the Detroits, who
was stopped at the door by a base-ball crank who eagerly
inquired the score. 'Four to three,' wearily responded
Dan, apparently thinking that his questioner would take
it for granted who were the winners. Then, as he passed
into the car, he espied Daboll and said to him: 'I wonder
if you people are as much annoyed as we are by fellows
talking shop.' This from a ball-player to an opera-singer
so astonished Daboll that he shrunk into a corner of the
car, and the elevator made four trips before he came to."

*
* *

"Just let me read you a specimen of 'English as she is
writ,' in the shape of a letter received the other day by
a dramatic agent here in town," said the Reporter. "It
reads like this: 'Kansas City, Mo., October 8, 1887. ——
—— (Agent). Dear Sir:—In answer to your adver in
N. Y. Clipper Oct 8th would say I seek a Musical and
Dramatical position Can lead as 1st Violin in Orchestra,
play Piano & Sing——(High Baritone Voice from
.[here is drawn a scale with one note down near the lower
cushion and another up near the second water-jump], a
sight reader, & experienced in good Amateur Dramatic

Cos—playing old men & eccentric Comedy parts, have the gift of imitating any well known actor with my voice & manners—Was Prompter & Musical leader to George Stange's Richard III., the Actor now travelling in Miln's Co am well read in all the leading plays & can memorize my parts very rapidly. I dress well, do not chew or dissipate, & to have experience with a GOOD company would be pleased to accept a very small salary & expenses at first. Is your Company a traveling one or Stationary—? Can send photo if wanted. If this interests you shall be glad to receive an answer—& to state any further particulars that may be desired. Yours Resply.' Now, what do you think of that for a literary production?"

*
* *

The Purveyor at this stage of the proceedings was cautiously approached by the speculative Agent, who informed him on the quiet that he had a sure thing in stocks, and he strongly advised him to purchase Western Union. "I bought some this morning," said the Purveyor. "The deuce you did! What did you pay for it?" was the Agent's astonished query. "Twenty-five cents for ten words," calmly replied the Purveyor; and the subsequent gloom was so dense that the casual adjournment of the Club could not be distinguished with the naked eye. In the language of the versatile Actor, it was "a body blow."

When the members of thé Turnover Club assembled
in the Usual Resort last evening, they found the Agent
explaining to the Purveyor a new and unique scheme.
He said that it had originally been unfolded to him by
Steve Richardson, who enacted the "haunted man" at
Kohl & Middleton's Dime Museum. When the Agent
said it was absolutely necessary that he should have a
glass of beer to perform the trick successfully, the Purveyor demurred, but finally his curiosity got the better
of him, and he drew the required beverage. The Agent
first took a sip of it, and then poured a small quantity
on the bar before him. Taking a small envelope from
his vest-pocket, he opened it and drew out a little
oblong piece of paper, and what appeared to be a section
of a blotting-pad. "Now," he said, immersing both in
the spilled beer, "I will reveal to you the features of
your future wife." The Actor murmured something
which sounded very much like "Rats!" but he watched
the mysterious proceeding with undisguised curiosity.
When the paraphernalia was thoroughly soaked, the
Agent proceeded to enfold the small bit of paper in the
blotting-pad, and then he tightly compressed the pulpy
mass between the palms of his hands. The suspense

7          (97)

was terrible. Pretty soon the Agent began to unfold the mysterious hunk of moisture, and from its inner recesses he proudly withdrew the water-logged bit of paper, and handed it over to the Purveyor. Upon its surface had appeared a face. It was the well-known face of the $10,000 base-ball beauty, Michael Jersey Kelly. "Is that my future wife?" queried the Purveyor, sarcastically. "I got things rather mixed," explained the Agent, who was quite discomfited at the failure of his wonderful scheme. "Steve gave me someone's future husband by mistake. They never mix futures over in the museum." "But I don't see why you couldn't have used water instead of beer," said the Purveyor. "Not and produce Mike Kelly's face," was the response.

\*\*\*

" While our 'Uncle Dick' Hooley was down East, last summer," put in the Manager, "he wrote Harry Powers, his assistant, to spend a little time and money in brightening up his pretty little play-house for the season; so Harry soon had men hard at work touching up the interior of the cosy theater. The frames of the chairs were repainted and renumbered, and Tommy Hooley was sent in to superintend this work. New box plans which showed the system of renumbering were procured, but they did not attract any particular attention until Nat Goodwin, the comedian, stepped up to the box-office window, the other day, to see how his sale of seats was for the evening. Tommy was on deck, and as he had just refused to give a box to the editor of the *Polish Wadski*, he was in a good humor. Nat gazed at the plan before him, and then said to Tom, 'Give me a stack of whites.' 'What for?' queried Tommy, in astonishment. 'Why, I want to play 'em on the "double O,"' was the response, and the comedian indicated one of two seats at the rear of the parquette. Then Tommy 'dropped,' and his chubby countenance gave birth to a wealth of smiles. When the men were renumbering the two sections on the sides of the parquette, they had run out of numbers, and had indicated the two remaining seats at the end of each section as O and OO. Each side looked like a roulette layout, and now when a newspaper man comes up and asks for two seats, Tommy folds up these O seats, and says, as he passes them out, 'The eagle bird, by chance.'"

\*\*

"Our young friend Fred Stinson is still here with Modjeska," said the Actor, "and his dog is registered with him at the hotel. It is a good dog, too—a greyhound, about a head taller than Fred, and a couple of sizes too large, remarkably well trained. In small towns, this sagacious animal attends to the gallery door, and will always ring for a pitcher of ice-water in the hotels every morning. It ought to be a good one, as it has cost Fred many sleepless nights, and hundreds of dollars in rewards. Charlie Powers, the business manager of the company, keeps himself in cigar money through the animal. When he strikes Fred in a town, he hires a boy for one dollar to steal the dog, and then realizes the ten-dollar reward offered invariably for its return, thereby clearing nine dollars on the deal. Fred likes greyhounds better than mastiffs. Two seasons ago, Modjeska had a couple of mastiffs to support her in a Russian play, and Fred cared for the animals off the stage, until one night, upon arriving in Chicago, they were in a hurry to reach the hotel, and dragged their little chaperon through the big snowdrifts to the Leland Hotel. After that experience, he sublet the brutes to an 'Uncle Tom' show, which subsequently changed Evas four times in one week. His new dog is very bright, and even laughed the other day when the holder of a bill-board pass addressed the Count Bozenta as 'Mr. Modjeska.'"

\* \*

"Your reference to Nat Goodwin a moment ago," remarked the Reporter, "reminds me that he told me the other day he was unaware that he was so well known in Chicago, especially over on the West Side." The Reporter, by the way, was in excellent humor, as his stylographic pen worked yesterday for the first time in two years, and he had partially allayed the excruciating rigors of corns by the purchase of shoes which resembled a pair of four-ounce boxing-gloves. "The other day," he continued, "Nat was riding on a West Side car, having purchased a ticket for an excursion to California avenue and return; and he said he was admiring the beautiful urban scenery, along with his own lithographs in the shop-windows, when suddenly his eye caught one of the largest lithographs, and he nearly fell from the car. There was his smiling countenance in a big, plate-glass window, and this counterfeit presentment of himself was topped by the word 'Liar,' in large, white letters. He said he wondered how they had 'got onto him' away out there; but as he drew nearer to investigate, he discovered that he had made a fatal error. The plate-glass belonged to a billiard-saloon, and across it was the word 'Billiards;' but his lithograph, which hung back of this, just caught the letters which made 'Liar.' Very much relieved at not having to slug a fellow-man, the comedian went inside and spent thirty cents playing billiards with himself for an hour."

"This is the season of the 'turkey actor,'" said the Agent. "What! Don't know what a 'turkey actor' is?" as the Proprietor arose to a question of information. "Why, you're not a voter, then. My boy, the 'turkey actors' blossom out about Thanksgiving-time, and go over the land discovering new towns. They create maps and open up wildernesses. Like the common turkey of the barn-yard, they flourish about the ides of November, though sometimes they last through the later holidays of the year. To the 'turkey actor' is awarded the credit of the discovery that 'one-night stands' can be played for a week, during which time 'all of the latest New York successes' can be presented by a band of players whose wardrobe is carried in a single hair trunk, and whose printing may be forwarded through the mails. The 'turkey actors' have encompassed the seemingly herculean task of playing 'Hamlet' with four people, all of whom are capable of 'playing brass' in the street parade. Their printing is selected from among the lurid assortment of 'stock-cuts' exhibited in show-printing houses; and often, by a little necessary doctoring with the types, the gorgeous wall-paper of the patent-medicine proprietor is made to do good service. In my travels on the edge of the map, I have witnessed 'stands of bills' that would fairly startle you. Imagine graphic printing announcing Hood's Celebrated Comedy Company, in the powerful, blood-regulating melodrama entitled 'Sarsaparilla; or, the Liver Regulators of Arizona,' the manager of which reserves the right to sell books of the play at fifty cents, or three bottles for one dollar—worth five dollars. Think of three-sheet posters reciting the merits of the brilliant young prima-donna, Miss Virginia Bitters, in comic opera, introducing the tonic-sol-fa system, and selling the tonic in the audience.  Or Nellie St. Jacobs' Burlesque Company, in the laughable extravaganza called 'Struck Oil;' and Siddell's Troubadours, in the farcical success, 'Don't be a Clam,' with the soap testimonials artfully altered to appear as indorsements of the show.  But the 'turkey actor' stops at nothing.  He hires his orchestra at the music-store, has his entire company assist in carrying it over to the town hall, puts his reserved seats on sale at the jewelry-store, and then takes tickets until it is time for him to dress for his part.  He never for a moment takes into consideration the population of a town.  He alights from the train at every stop.  If there is only a water-tank there, he lets the water out and plays in the tank, at popular prices.  And when the walking grows bad, he sinks into oblivion, to reappear along with the President's next Thanksgiving proclamation.  Verily, the 'turkey actor' is a great institution."

\* \*
\*

"One of the boys was telling me, the other day," said the Night Clerk, "of an experience that Ned Thorne had with his play, 'The Black Flag,' last summer.  He had collected around him a small company, and was engaged in putting in a portion of the hot spell in traveling over the coast circuit and entertaining the people of seaside summer resorts.  One night, they reached Red Bank, N. J., and played in a remodeled roller-skating rink, which had numerous windows on all sides.  In the middle of the second act, the fire-bell over in Asbury Park sounded an alarm, and the people who composed the small audience of some thirty or forty began tip-toeing out to see the blaze.  At this, Ned stopped the performance, stepped to the foot-lights, and said:  'Ladies and gentlemen, don't be alarmed; there is a window for each one of you.' "

"It is said that every household has its skeleton in the closet," remarked the Counsellor, "and our establishment here appears to be no exception to that rule, though our skeleton is not in the closet, as it should be, but right out on the lunch-counter;" and he gazed pensively at the bony architecture composing all that remained mortal of a once proud gobbler. "That 'turk,'" he went on, "has long outlived its usefulness, and if the Proprietor were to do what is right, he would lose no time in filing away, in the lowest pigeon-hole of his ash-barrel, that awful wreck of what was, on Thanksgiving morning, an alluring bait for the epicures who demolished it. The feature of the Proprietor's Thanksgiving lunch, by the way, was an immense platter of spaghetti. In the successful consumption of this Italian fruit a man requires an iron nerve, an unerring aim, and a fork with a far-reaching and all-absorbing tine. To a muddled individual with a common, every-day fork, spaghetti is by all odds the most elusive food in the Home Cook-Book. He toys with a spear of it, carefully balances it upon his German-silver prodder, and starts it toward his anxious mouth, only to see it uncoil its slimy folds and flop back into its native element. It was a bright idea of the Proprietor, that dish, because it lasted so long. Made his afternoon and evening customers nervous, though, and hurt his bar-trade somewhat."

\* \*
\*

"That Steve Richardson, who gave me the hidden photo of Mike Kelly," put in the Agent, "is the man with the copper-toed voice who uses it to dilate upon the merits of the artists in the dime museum stage performances. He was telling me the other day how the craze for fame before the foot-lights affected some of his stage hands. One of these is a husky young German called

Fritz, who heard of the museum's offer of $1,000 to any man who could equal Herr Dodretti's feat of raising a live horse with his teeth, and who secretly resolved to go into training for the prize. At the museum, last week, were the two strong men, Samson and Hercules, whose crowning achievement was the lifting of a three-hundred-pound dumb-bell. If you have ever dallied with a dumb-bell of this growth, you will admit its sedentary habits. Well, during a performance once, and while Steve was on the stage engaged in oratorically paving the way for a serio-comic singer, he was startled by a frightful crash, and he ran behind the scenes to see what was up. He found something down instead. It was Fritz. In juggling with the mastodon dumb-bell he had inadvertently allowed it to fall across his neck, and there he reclined, with his eyes popping out of his head, his tongue directed toward the zenith, and his arms and legs gyrating wildly. Steve attempted to lift the mass of iron, but only succeeded in getting it up far enough to drop back on poor Fritz's neck. Then a pair of song and dance men lent four hands, but it would not budge, in spite of their great reputation as budgers. Finally, Steve had to send down to the dressing-rooms for Samson and Hercules, who were playing checkers for the prospective beer, and Fritz was taken out of bondage. He is still stuck on the show business, and the manager says that, if the crease on his neck does not fade out, he will dress him up as a cow-boy and bill him as Arizona Jim, who had been lynched in New Mexico for lifting horses without the aid of his teeth."

\* \*
\*

" I see that Captain Anson is to open a racquet court here," remarked the Actor. " What's that? No, I mean an entirely different sort of a racquet. This is a sort of a

society game.   That will let the Manager out, as he is
not a society duck.   He thinks he is, though.   But I
remember of his going to a wedding last winter, and he
handed his invitation to the Senegambian who was 'on
the door,' saying, 'How's the house?' and bowing himself in.   When he went out to make a bluff call for his
carriage he said, 'I don't need a check, do I?'   That's
the kind of a society duck he is.   There goes that electric light again.   Guess we'd better adjourn;" and the
Club filed out, softly singing, "We're Going Home to
Dy-na-mo."

It was the Reporter who was in the very midst of a sad state of unrest when the members of the Turnover Club tiptoed into the Usual Resort last evening. He stated that he had been in his customary hard luck. At a recent interesting evening session at draw poker he had been sadly worsted in two successive jack-pots of goodly proportions, and only that day he had declined to take out an accident policy in a company which guaranteed $2,500 for the loss of two hands. Had he accepted the insurance agent's tempting offer before the session, he would have quit more than even. This was but one instance of the manner in which a cruel fate awarded him that discouraging experience ycleped "the razzle-dazzle." He said he would be perfectly willing to bet that if he had been the jail barber last Thursday, the suicided anarchist, Louis Lingg, would have applied to him for a dry shampoo while the dynamite cartridge was concealed in his hair. His wife had been told by the milkman, the Reporter went on, that the anarchist had departed this life through the agency of a cigarette rolled with dynamite, and when he reached home she began to lecture him on the evil consequences of the awful cigarette habit. That was her one great weakness, he said.

If he incautiously complained of a ferocious corn, or found fault because there was a button off of his shirt, she always declared that it was due to cigarette-smoking. All this did not appear to terrify the Reporter, though, for while he was telling of it he ignited one of those vicious little paper pipes, and calmly allowed the deadly nicotine to chip away at what was remaining of his left lung.

\* \*
\*

"You know Mark Sullivan, of Hoyt's 'Rag Baby' Company, don't you?" queried the Agent. "Plays the Irish policeman. Well, several times last season, when Frank Daniels was sick, Mark was called upon to play 'Old Sport.' He's a clever comedian, and he did it remarkably well. When Daniels seceded, this season, Mark approached Hoyt and asked for a show to play the part. 'I have already played it,' he said, 'and the audiences did not ask to have their money refunded.' Mr. Hoyt said he granted that, but the fact was he did not fancy the name of Sullivan as a star. 'What's the matter with Sir Arthur Sullivan?' asked Mark, hotly, and as Hoyt could not answer that argument, he walked away. His speaking of names, however, reminds me of the expedient of Charlie Davis, a brother of poor 'Jumbo' Davis, who used to travel in advance of the Forepaugh show. The incident happened in the days before the Inter-State Commerce Bill reared its awful head and crushed out theatrical railroad passes. Davis, who has a slight impediment in his speech, had to carry many heavy bill trunks, which called for large amounts in the way of extra baggage, so he figured to shut off this drain. He was traveling through the South at the time, and the accommodating passenger agents down in that country made his passes read, 'Pass Charles Davis and bill boxes.' He could not get a pass for his assistant, however, so when a train conductor would approach the pair and ask for tickets, Charlie would hand out the pass and say: 'I am Charles D-d-davis, and th-this is B-b-bill B-b-boxes,' pointing to his assistant. It worked like a charm, and this same assistant, who is now ahead of a minstrel show, has been known ever since as Bill Boxes."

\*\*\*

"Charlie Gardner, the German comedian, is rehearsing his company here this week," said the Actor. "I happened to run across him the other day, and he told me a story of a certain young serio-comic singer who had ambition. She desired to elevate the tone of her act, and sing pathetic ballads. Well, the management allowed her to do so, and she started in on her new career by warbling that delicious morceau, 'Close the Shutters, Willie's Dead.' She had no time to procure appropriate wardrobe, so she went on in her serio-comic togs—short dress and the traditional fan hanging from a ribbon at her waist. The ballad went very well, and she secured a big reception. This so elated her that in the last chorus she forgot herself, and thought only of the old days. Grabbing her fan, she shot it open with a bang, assumed a marching step in quick time, and minced across the stage, singing 'Close the Shutters, Willie's Dead,' to a very lively tune. The effect may be imagined. The next day the managers informed her that she had better go back to straight serio-comic business. One of Gardner's orchestra, by the way," resumed the Actor, "went to Charlie early last season, when they were out on the road, and said that as he had not sent any money home to his wife, he desired to send her something. 'Well, my boy,' said Charlie, 'send her the route and the programme.'"

"Did any of you hear how Billy Rice, 'Hoochy-Coochy,' was bunkoed by 'Yank' Adams, out in Denver. last week?" asked the Agent. "Well, it appears that 'Yank' was out there on business, and he ran across Billy, who was with Thatcher, Primrose & West's Minstrels. On the first night of the performance, Rice exploited his old, moss-covered gag about the bottom falling out of his hack while he was out riding and his being obliged to run eight miles inside of the vehicle in consequence. On this particular occasion he told that his trip had been made from the Rosedale lots—a new suburban resort of Denver which was being heavily advertised there at the time. The next morning the owner of these lots went around to the hotel to see if he could not induce Rice to use the name of his resort in the story all through the week, and in front of the caravansary he came upon 'Yank,' who sported a striped shirt, a big diamond, and a plug hat. 'One of the minstrels?' queried the lot-owner, approaching him. 'Yes,' replied Adams, coolly, 'I'm the manager.' Then the man inquired how much it would cost him to have Billy Rice advertise his lots during the week. 'I was just going around to see you about that,' said 'Yank.' 'We always do that. It will cost you $100.' This was too much, and they finally compromised on $50—$25 down, and the balance at the end of the week, and 'Yank' pocketed $25. Meeting Rice at breakfast, 'Yank' told him that the owner of the Rosedale lots was a cousin of his, and had been greatly pleased at their mention. Billy said he was very glad of it, and to oblige 'Yank's' cousin he would use the 'gag' all week. This he did faithfully, and 'Yank' drew the other $25 on time, earning his hotel-bill. To this day, Billy Rice does not know that he worked all of one week for 'Yank' Adams."

"The other day," put in the Manager, "Jack Moynihan was telling me of a funny experience he had once in Champaign, Illinois, with a company playing in that little town. The star of this troupe was Josie Crocker, a favorite in Chicago in the old museum days, and Jack was the stage-manager. It was a small company, and they played a full week in little towns, changing the bill nightly. In Champaign, on Saturday night, Jack went up to the theater to see that everything was in readiness for the announced performance of 'Camille' that evening. When he went upon the stage, his eyes were riveted by a ghastly sight. Against the wall stood a large coffin, with white satin linings and silver mountings. Hastily summoning the property-man, Jack demanded to know what this meant. 'Why, you told me to get it,' was the startling reply. 'Told you to get it?' wonderingly queried the dumbfounded Moynihan. 'Yes, you told me to get a "casket" for the last act of "Camille."' When the astonished stage-manager regained his breath, he told the property-man that what he meant was a casket for *Camille's* jewels."

\* \*
\*

"I met Ned Kohl, of Kohl & Middleton, the museum men, the other afternoon," said the Actor, "and he told me that he had just returned from Cincinnati, whither he had been called by an urgent telegram. You know these museum men own a place in Cincinnati also, and the telegram was an appeal from their local manager for Kohl to come down there at once, as there was trouble. When he arrived, he said he found that the landlord of the Gibson House had insisted upon charging double rates for Millie Christine, the two-headed colored girl who was playing with them there. Ned claimed that she was only one person, and should be charged for as such, but the landlord insisted that she had two mouths to feed, and that she ate as much as any two of his guests. Kohl replied that this was all bosh, as the girls had only one stomach between them, and he did not propose to be robbed. It was finally arranged that they should be charged one and one-half fare for the round trip, and then Kohl hastened back here to Chicago to make an agreed hotel rate for the twins, who come here next week."

*⁎*

"Frank Lane, of John T. Raymond's company, was telling yesterday of an Elks' social session which he attended in the East," remarked the Professor. "It was to be quite an affair, and Frank Moran, the well-known minstrel man, came many miles to preside. He makes an inimitable chairman on such occasions, and this was no exception to the rule. He announced each number on the programme with some witty remark, and finally he said: 'We come now to one whom we may aptly term our "chestnut brother," he being old enough to be the grandfather of anyone here; he will give us a recitation.' The brother referred to arose and stated that if he was the 'chestnut brother' he would recite a 'chestnut'—'The Charge of the Light Brigade.' For the benefit of those who had never heard it, he first explained that of the gallant 'six hundred' who went into the fight, but sixty came out of it alive. Then he recited the poem in a stirring manner that called forth enthusiastic and prolonged applause. Finally, Chairman Moran rapped for order and said: 'Brother ——, there appears to be a general desire on the part of the brethren present that you kill that other sixty!'"

*⁎*

"Our friend George Schiller, of the 'Evangeline' company, has been a real theater actor for a long time," said the Manager, "but it is only lately that he has taken to burlesque. He used to be in the legitimate, where he played heavy parts, though if you'd ever see him on the scales you'd never think that. Yes, I remember that one season he was doing the 'leading heavies' with Weird & Awful's Barn-stormers, traveling through territory where lynch-law was frowned upon by enlightened communities of the 'one-night-stand' order. Our fellow townsman, William Ananias McConnell, was also a member of the company, playing the 'leading juveniles' and the hotels. The repertoire of the company consisted of 'The Hidden Hand,' 'Hamlet,' 'She Stoops to Conquer,' 'Frost Bitten' (from which 'Storm Beaten' was plagiarized), and 'Pajamas.' The management endeavored to induce John L. Sullivan to appear in his master-piece, 'A Scrap on Paper,' but he refused. Salary did not stand in the way, as there wasn't enough of it, but he declined to go into training for the company's long jumps. Well, the troupe struck Michigan, and stopped at Muskallonge to present 'The Hidden Hand.' It had not been presented there since a Chicago gambler had been shot for doing it, six years before. Schiller played *Black Donald*, the wicked villain of the piece, and his 'make-up' was something frightful. His countenance resembled the collar of an astrakhan coat. Owing to the fact that there were no town-halls in some of the places the company paused at, the company carried its own opera-house and played under canvas. As the stage was but thirteen inches from the ground, and *Black Donald* had to fall through a trap, it was necessary for Schiller to hire the village sexton to dig below the trap a hole large enough for his complete concealment when he fell through it. Schiller and McConnell roomed together, and the day they played in Muskallonge, Schil-

8

ler arose in the morning first, thereby securing the vest.
This naturally piqued McConnell. He hastily swallowed
his supper that night and hurried over to the tent. No
one was inside excepting the property-man, who was
engaged in filling the foot-lights with kerosene, and Will
swore him to secrecy over a bad cigar. Then he went
outside and readily recognized two of the village 'kids,'
who are always eager and willing to carry water for the
elephant when the circus comes to town. He promised
them two tickets to the show, and thus induced them to
fill up *Black Donald's* pit with water from the town-
pump. The performance went along smoothly until it
came the heavy villain's time to fall through the trap.
There was a splash, a gurgling outcry, and the water
flew in all directions. 'Let him alone!' yelled McConnell from the wings. 'He's got to come up three times!'
But the curtain was rung down, and *Black Donald* was
wrung out. 'Well, McConnell didn't make much out of
it,' said Schiller, when the story was told on him the
other day, 'for it ruined the vest, and neither of us could
wear it after that—it was too small for Commodore
Nutt!'"

\*\*\*

"Supper is now ready in the imperial palace dining-
car!" shouted the Purveyor, as he threw open both lids
of the cracker and cheese casket and pushed the dish of
olives toward the members. Some time was consumed
in the discussion of these viands, after which the Purveyor turned off the gas, made a record of the state of
the meter, and closed up.

# XII.

When the Turnover Club assembled at the Usual Resort last evening, the members resolved to wear the customary badge of mourning on the left arm for a period of thirty days. It appeared that the Agent had, during the week, fractured the solemn pledge he had registered, by spending some three days and nights in what is variously termed a "toot" in musical circles, a "bat" among ball-players, and a "time" by the public at large. On Friday evening, his remains had been turned over to the Proprietor, who is Grand Pronged Horn in the Chicago Lodge of Elks, and he accomplished the difficult task of bringing him to. When he discovered his whereabouts, he strenuously insisted on loading up again; but the Grand Pronged Horn—always true to the sacred trust reposed in him— told the Purveyor not to fill his order. A compromise was finally effected by the two indulging in seltzer lemonades, in payment for which the Agent tendered a silver dollar and directed the Purveyor to punch out two drinks, as it was a commutation coin. In consequence of his extended debauch, the "advance announcer" was in possession of a very able breath—one of those respirations which carves its initials upon the bark of the

great oak Memory, and when once fully realized can
never be forgotten.   A clove had no more effect upon it
than has a drop of pure water upon the stalwart bosom
of Chicago's beautiful river, and a cassia-bud was to it as
the perfume of a single Eastern lily in the atmosphere
of the Union Stock Yards.   Whatever might have been
said about that breath, it was very certain that " the
flowers that bloom in the spring, tra-la, had nothing to do
with the case."   And this was the reason why the Agent
was in bad odor when the Club assembled last evening.

\* \*
\*

"Are you acquainted with Al Johnson, of Cleveland ? "
queried the Manager.   " No ?   Well, then, half of your
life has been a perfect blank.   He's a jolly good fellow,
and he has just returned from ' the other side,' whither
he went with his friends ' Doc ' Beeman and Will Hoey, of
Evans and Hoey, the comedians.   While in London, the
trio visited the Alhambra, and witnessed the magnificent
' Ballet of All Nations' which is being presented there.
They enjoyed the spectacle hugely; but when the bevy
of pretty girls tripped out upon the stage bearing the
American flag, the trio arose as one man and howled in
chorus.   It was the first time that Al Johnson had been
overcome by patriotism, but he shouted until he was
black in the face; and Will Hoey stood up alongside
of him and yelled, at the top of his voice: ' There she is;
God bless her !   Here's to America, the land of the free;
the home of Al Johnson, Doc Beeman, and me ! '   You
can just imagine the effect of this on an English audience.   Johnson tells this, and he also tells a story Hoey
relates on one of his ' down East ' neighbors, to illustrate
the generosity of some of those thrifty ' Yanks.'   A
woman went out into her front yard and saw a tramp,
ragged and dirty, down on his knees eating the grass on

the lawn. She asked him if he was really as hungry as all that, and when he sadly replied that he really was, she said, compassionately: ' Poor fellow; come around in the back yard—the grass is much longer there.' "

* * *

" Billy Crane, the comedian, is here this week," put in the Actor, " and he is looking remarkably well ; though it is a fact that he has lost nineteen pounds since he began to play *Falstaff*. The big stomach-pad which he wears weighs about a ton, and he is obliged to have it sent to the hotel every day to have the perspiration dried out of it. Why, at the end of each performance he finds that the perspiration has soaked through his heavy russet boots. If anyone earns his bread by the sweat of his brow, I think Crane does. But then he makes it all up during the summer vacation. He and his partner in crime, Robson, have houses in the theatrical colony at Cohasset, Massachusetts, on the seashore, and he enjoys life there on his yacht, the ' Viff.' His old skipper is a great character, and can do anything on shipboard, from guiding a rudder to cooking. One day, while on a cruise along the shore, the yacht went aground, and the skipper set about getting her off by securing a good purchase with the hauling away. So he went forward, grabbed a portion of the rigging, and threw the anchor ahead with a mighty heave. Just as he threw, the rigging parted, and, in the excitement of the moment, the skipper neglected to let go of the anchor; so he brought up at the bottom of Massachusetts Bay. He had just reached the surface and pulled himself aboard of the yacht again, when he discovered floating upon the surface of the water, near by, the good cigar which he had lighted just before he fell overboard. As he reached over to get it, his foot slipped and he slid into the drink

again. Then he said they had better anchor the yacht
and wait for the next tide; so he calmly rolled up his
pants, tucked the anchor under his arm, and waded out
until he found a spot where it could 'catch on.' All of
this time Mr. Crane and his guests were rolling about
the deck of the yacht in convulsions of merriment."

* *
*

" I was informed recently, on the very best of author-
ity," said the Counsellor, " that our young cigar friend,
William Y. Daniels, was about to indulge in a well-earned
vacation. A friend was urging him to accompany him
to the wild and woolly West on a pleasure-trip. At first,
William declared that he would not go, under any circumstances. 'But think of it, Bill,' put in his friend;
'you can hunt Indians!' 'I haven't lost any Indians,'
responded William; but he had. About a year ago, Mr.
Daniels purchased a lignum-vitæ savage with a toma-
hawk in one hand and a bunch of Waterbury cigars in
the other, and perched him just outside the door of his
fine-cut emporium. The next morning the Indian had
disappeared. Nothing daunted, Mr. Daniels went out to
the reservation, on Clybourne avenue, and secured a
duplicate savage; but the kidnaper took him, also, a night
or two later. This was getting pretty tiresome; but Mr.
Daniels drew another card, and this time he had his
bogus noble red man firmly spiked to the stone sidewalk.
There he remained until the elements had made him look
a little careworn; and one day a man came along and
offered to regild the untutored savage for a consideration
of ten dollars. To this proposition Mr. Daniels consented, and the figure was carted away. He has not seen
the third Indian from that day to this; and now he is
disgusted with the aborigines, and will not even go to a
Wild West show."

"Frank Lane, of Robert Downing's company, thinks that Chicago is one of the greatest summer resorts on earth," said the Night Clerk. "Since he has been here he has wilted, on an average, eight collars per day, in consequence of which he has vainly endeavored to obtain professional rates at a laundry. You are of course aware that he hovers in the neighborhood of two hundred avoirdupois, and he declared last week that his avoirdupois did not have much the best of Chicago's Fahrenheit. Frank is the 'understudy' of Muldoon, the wrestler, and plays the *Fighting Gaul* when 'Mul' is sick. The other day, the two started out in search of a place where they could go into training. Muldoon intends to train Frank down to his fighting weight, and when he finds suitable quarters he will observe the following rigid course of training: Eleven A. M., arise and push annunciator for cracked ice and a hose; 11.30 A. M., breakfast, consisting of clam cocktail, gin ditto, and sour olives; twelve M., purchase one pool on a short horse at Saratoga; 12.30 P. M., watch ticker for result of race; 12.33 P. M., tear up pool-ticket; 12.50 P. M., another breakfast as before; two P. M., watch the base-ball scores on the ticker and talk about the games; six P. M., supper, consisting of Welsh rarebit and hard-boiled eggs; eight P. M., take in some show; —— P. M., all the other places closed up; —— P. M., go to bed. Muldoon thinks that this course of training will put Frank in good condition. I wouldn't wonder at all if it did."

*<br>* *

"Talking about training," remarked the Reporter, "reminds me of a good one I heard the other day on Johnny Neumeister, the ex-City Clerk. He went out to the West Side Driving Park a few days ago, with a party of friends, to see some horses tried; and after the trial, they were all sitting on the club-house veranda, talking of sporting matters in general, when John said he would bet $20 that he could beat anyone in the party in a run around the track. He is considerable of an all-round athlete, and at first no one seemed disposed to accept his challenge; but finally a gentleman in the party produced a friend whom he said was a runner, and declared his willingness to back him to the extent of $20. Accordingly, the money was put up, the men stripped to the waist, and at an agreed signal both darted off. They ran together to the half-mile, where John's opponent took the lead. John was just a mite winded, and he yelled to the other man that if he would allow him to win they would divide the stakes; but the other man paid no attention to him. This nettled John, and shutting his teeth hard, he muttered, 'I'll beat you now, anyway.' Down the home-stretch both men came at a terrific pace, and John finished a winner by about three feet. When he was told subsequently that his opponent was deaf and dumb, he understood why no attention was paid to his proposition at the half-mile pole; and when the mute learned how he had been approached, he wrote on his cuff that he would have been only too glad to have accepted the proposition, if he had heard it. John bought the wine."

\* \*

"Speaking of languages," said the Agent, "do you know why Warren Leland, the hotel man, has used such language against the proposed toboggan-slide on the lake-front up in his neighborhood? No? Well, I'll tell you. Leland is a man who always sees all there is to be seen wherever he goes. Last winter he took in the St. Paul ice carnival, and in an evil moment he allowed some of his friends to persuade him to indulge in a ride

on one of the devices.   He did not have any canton flannel bathing-suit or worsted cap to wear, but his friends
assured him that made no appreciable difference, as per-
sons not in costume were allowed on the floor.   When
they let go of Leland's toboggan on the top of the slide,
there were seven good-sized men on it, and Mr. Leland
was pulling the stroke-oar.   Someone gave ' Gallagher'
the necessary signal, and he 'let 'er go.'   To this day,
Mr. Leland declares, that if he could identify that man
Gallagher, he would lick him on sight.

" Well, the toboggan began its downward career.   Mr.
Leland endeavored to catch breath enough to inquire
of the man directly behind him at what time they were
due at Council Bluffs, but he could not do so.   Then his
foot slipped down off of the perch, and his right pants-
leg began to scoop up snow at an alarming rate.   Mr.
Leland said, afterward, that he should not have minded
this in the least if the snow hadn't annoyed the man
behind him by blowing into his face as it came out of the
back of his neck.   When the machine came to a stand-
still, Mr. Leland told his friends that if they didn't mind
he would walk over to the Milwaukee avenue cars and
ride down-town, which he proceeded to do without delay.
And that is the reason why he kicks about having a
toboggan-slide in his vicinity."

*  *
*

There was a flash, a loud report, and the Agent jerked
the débris of a shattered cigar from between his lips
and savagely cast it toward the other extremity of the
bar.   He was ghastly pale, and decidedly angry.   He
said that if he knew who gave him that loaded cigar, he
would certainly perpetrate an awful deed.   The Purveyor declared that it was the fault of the Agent himself,
as everyone plainly saw him strike a match, light the

fuse, and subsequently throw the bomb. The Agent protested that it was no laughing matter, as he had heart disease, and the Reporter, who was about to expend a quarter in the entertainment of the members, wisely refrained, in fear that two such severe shocks in succession might hasten the end; so the Club put on its hats and adjourned, there being no further business.

# XIII.

When the members of the Turnover Club answered to roll-call in the Usual Resort last evening, there was a noticeable change apparent in each one of them. Their bearing was marked by more dignity, *qui vive, bon mot,* and *esprit de corps.* When the Manager summoned the Purveyor, he shouted: "Come hither, slave!" instead of "Same as I had before;" and the Reporter went out to the cigar-case, rapped sharply upon the glass with his last nickel, and cried: "What ho, within there!" Then when the Proprietor emerged and procured the desired cigarettes, the Reporter told him to "put it on the ice." The Agent scared the life out of a messenger-boy by grabbing his coat-collar and yelling in his ear, "Quick, boy—the message, the dispatch!" with a very Butte City Richelieu expression of countenance. In fact, an air of tragedy pervaded the entire assemblage. The Agent explained this change to the apparently mystified Counsellor by saying that "the comics" were about to leave town, and that they were to be entertained for a season by "the tragics." The companies of both Louis James and Robert Downing were here rehearsing, and the stage-carpenters were hard at work copper-toeing the scenery. This was why the members deemed it only fitting and proper to cast aside the air of unseemly hilarity which had characterized the recent visit of the burnt-corkers, and don the more appropriate expression of dignified woe. Then the members arranged themselves at the bar of the Purveyor and proceeded to order one Roman punch, one Grecian sour, one wassail, and three stirrup-cups, the latter with very little froth. "To the health of our king!" cried the Actor, waving aloft one of the stirrup-cups and spilling about a gill of its contents down the Manager's neck; but the Agent sadly marred the effect of this fitting tragic illusion by remarking, "Let 'er go, Gallagher," as he quaffed his Roman punch.

\*\*\*

"Speaking of tragedy and tragedians," said the Actor, "reminds me of a good story on our friend Will McConnell. While he was 'on the road' once with John McCullough, he arrived with the star and company at a certain town, went up to the best hotel in the place, and affixed his autograph to the register. When the clerk turned the big book around and saw the signature, he was all smiles at once, and at his bidding seven bell-boys made a grab for Will's small grip. He was shown up to a fine parlor, with bath and bed-room off, on the second floor, and was soon comfortably seated before a cheerful fire which blazed in the grate. 'They must know me here,' he mused, as he wondered just a little at the great amount of attention shown him; and he sent down an invitation to the other young men in the company to come up and view his elegant quarters, and put their feet on the marble-topped table. Pretty soon, the same seven bell-boys who had grabbed at Will's grip came up and threw the whole party out into

the hall, while the head porter said to McConnell:
'Why in —— don't you write your name so that 'a
man can read it? We thought you were John McCullough!'"

\*\*

"When McConnell was out in advance of 'Furnished
Rooms,'" put in the Manager, "poor Joe Gulick used to
send him money packages to every town, in order to create an impression on the local managers. On the outside
would be marked some such amount as $480, while
inside would be probably a ten-dollar bill and some
newspaper clippings. These 'bluff' packages staggered
the hotel men, though, and Will used to come pretty near
owning the hotels. This company playing 'Furnished
Rooms' was one of the companies then managed by
Joe Gulick and John Blaisdell. At first, they were called
'Guaranteed Attractions;' but later on, when financial
troubles beset the management, they became known as
'Garnisheed Attractions.' Gulick and Blaisdell both had
desk-room up in Charlie McConnell's office. When a
messenger-boy would come in with a telegram for either
one of them, the other would take it, tear it open hurriedly, and then, if it was marked 'Collect,' he would
glance at the envelope and say: 'My boy, this is a mistake; I thought it was for me, but it is for my partner
instead. He is out of town just now.' And the messenger-boy would take the telegram back to the office. In
this ingenious way, the two hard-pressed managers
received and read all of their telegrams without the
annoying accompaniment of paying for them."

\*\*

"Arthur Cambridge, the dramatic agent, is about to
rig up a new scheme," said the Actor. " Heretofore, in
his agency, he has booked professionals' names, lines of

business, and addresses only.  Now he intends to write
their dimensions in the record.  One day last week a
man rushed up into his actor-foundry and said that Mrs.
Langtry wanted a good actor, and that she wanted him
right away, as a rehearsal was going on.  Arthur recom-
mended the best artist he had in sight, and sent him
over to the theater.  He returned shortly, and in answer
to Colonel Cambridge's question, he said: 'Well, I went
over there and reported myself.  She looked me over
carefully from head to foot, and then remarked, " Oh,
you'll never do at all—you won't fit the costume." '
Arthur thought that if the Jersey Lily had wanted an
actor to fit a costume, she should have at least sent him
the chest measurement with the order.  However, he
summoned another artist, who had just returned from
playing *Romeos* and *Claudes* in Janesvilles and Topekas,
and sent him over.  Pretty soon he returned, beaming
with gladsome smiles, and exclaimed, triumphantly:
' Well, I've got an engagement—I fit the costume.'  And
Arthur congratulated himself that he had not yet got
down to running a misfit actors' parlors."

\*
\*\*

" Did you hear what the Proprietor's wife had to stand
from him after he returned home from our last meeting?" asked the Night Clerk.  "Well, you know when
he left here he was feeling pretty gay, and when he
struck the bed it was not many moments before he was
sound asleep.  Along about one A. M., his wife awoke him
by a startling series of energetic punches.  She, by the
by, is one of those thrifty housewives who seldom forgets
any detail of household arrangement.  'Charlie,' she
said, 'I do believe I have forgotten to put that mackerel
in soak.'  The Proprietor, suddenly aroused, yawned
lazily, stretched himself, and drawled out, half-asleep,

'Never mind, my dear—I don't think you could get much on it, anyway.' When his wife taxed him about it the next morning, he denied having made any such remark."

\*\*\*

" I see that Jim Meade is in our midst," remarked the Agent. " Hear about his accident in Philadelphia, recently? No? Well, he hit a piece of ice one day, and when he started to arise from the sidewalk he discovered that a leg was broken. He was conveyed to his room in the hotel, and when the doctor came in, he juggled with the disabled member, said ' Two dollars, please,' and told Jim that he would be obliged to remain horizontal for at least three months. This was cheerful news for him. Well, his friends heard of his mishap, and every night Harry Dixey brought up a party after his show and spent the night with Jim, making him forget about his fractured limb with funny stories. During the day, he used to doze off occasionally, but the slightest touch would awaken him. One afternoon, he started up suddenly out of a refreshing nap, and discovered a very funereal-looking man bending over him, wearing ghastly green goggles and having in his hand a tape-measure. 'What are you doing?' queried Jim, in a rather dazed way. 'I'm only measuring you for a crutch,' was the response. ' Oh, go ahead then,' was Jim's next remark. ' I thought you might be sizing me up for a coffin;' and then he rolled over, and was soon sound asleep again. It takes a good deal to disturb Jim's rest."

\*\*\*

" I went up to call on the Counsellor the other day, and I am now consulting him as to the advisability of suing the owner of his building for damages," remarked the Professor. " You know where he's located, and his office is much nearer the roof than the basement. I did not suspect any plot, and I went in to take the elevator. Just here, allow me to tell you never to take that elevator, unless someone hands it to you on a salver. I plunked the annunciator, and stood in front of the wire doors waiting for the cage to descend from above. When it arrived, it brought with it a fearful gust of wind, that took off my new derby and slammed it violently against the opposite wall. When I recovered it, and entered the waiting cage, I saw the young man in charge sit down upon a lever, and then I certainly thought that I was going where I could read the answer in the stars without any great difficulty. However, the young man pulled out a stop at the fourth floor, and I escaped. After I had consulted the Counsellor, I offered to take him out and purchase the usual retaining fee; and together we entered the cyclone in the elevator shaft. When the boy sat on the lever again, I thought the man on the roof had allowed his foot to slip, and that we would certainly bore a hole into the Western Hemisphere in our mad career. It felt, when the cage struck bottom and disgorged us, as though I had left my breakfast up on the third floor. Every tenant in that building is obliged to wear his hair *a la Pompadour*, as the rapid rides in this awful elevator make it stand on end. It's a wonder!"

\* \*
\*

"Frank Lane is still in our midst, I see," said the Reporter. "The other day I heard him talking to a friend whose wife had recently presented him with a new baby. The happy parent was praising the many good qualities of the infant, and he remarked that the little one had red cheeks, like his. 'Not from the same cause, though,' said Frank. 'His are from the rays of the sun, while yours are from the raise of the glass.' Clever, wasn't it?"

\*\*\*

"Young Frank Moynihan was telling me, the other day, of a recent experience he had out on the road with a barn-storming 'Monte Cristo' company," put in the Proprietor. "They played around in the cheaper theaters, and one night they appeared in a place where drinks were dispensed in the auditorium. The man who played *Edmond Dantes* had killed the first of his three enemies, and had shouted 'One!' When he slew his second victim, he yelled 'Two!' and as a couple of his fingers shot out toward the audience, as an accompaniment to the exclamation, an active German waiter, who was vigilantly patrolling the center aisle, accepted it as an order, and cried 'Zwei!' and a moment later he attempted to scale the foot-lights and reach the star with two foaming beers."

\*\*\*

"This man George H. Woods, who styles himself 'The Somewhat Different Comedian,' and who is doing a monologue with Haverly's company this week, is a clever performer," remarked the Agent. "He is a man of superior education, too, having been trained for the priesthood, and possesses a remarkable flow of language. If you should see him off the stage, you would never take him for a burnt-cork artist. The other night I met him, and he was telling me of a friend of his who had spent many years of his life as an English cavalry trooper. He was an exceedingly lazy man, and used to curse the blatant bugler who tooted the reveille at 5.30 A. M. daily. At the last moment he would spring from his cot, jump into his uniform, and always appear on the parade-ground not a moment too soon. For

9

years he was obliged to do this; but at last a grandmother
of his died, leaving him a snug fortune, and he purchased
his discharge.   Then he hired a cozy house on London's
outskirts, furnished it comfortably, and employed an
old, superannuated army bugler to come beneath his
window every morning and sound the reveille.   When
it reached the ear of the retired trooper, he would arise
from his downy couch, glare out of the casement at the
bugler, cry, 'You go to ——!' and then return to his bed.
He was getting even for years of discomfort."

* * *

"Digby Bell, the comic opera comedian, is a great
base-ball crank, as you all know," said the Counsellor.
"He is a great favorite in Philadelphia, and, when singing
there, is always in demand as umpire for the amateur
games.   One day last summer he took the usual chances,
and, with umpire indicator in hand, he umpired a game
between the Philadelphia 'Fats' and 'Leans.'   The star
'Fat' was Charlie Jackson, a local mammoth, who keeps a
liquid grocery store, and it has been said of him that,
in all of his business experience, he has never once
walked home or ridden home in a street-car, invariably
going in a cab.   Well, Jackson was finally assisted to
the bat, and through some mischance he reached first
base.   Then the 'Leans' began to fire the ball all over
Philadelphia and her beautiful suburbs, and meantime
Jackson toiled around to third base.   Here he was
grabbed by the rest of the 'Fats' and a cab was driven
onto the field.   The star 'Fat' was pried into it and
driven in triumph to the plate.   'There,' exclaimed one
of the 'Fats,' 'we've driven you home, Charlie, because
we didn't want you to break your record!'   Digby
declared that the run was earned, and that it was due
entirely to superior coaching on the part of the cabby."

"I do hate most awfully to spring a 'chestnut' on this gathering," interrupted the Purveyor, "but I feel obliged to inform you all that our closing hour is midnight." So they went around just once, and then the Proprietor rang down the curtain.

# XIV.

When the members of the Turnover Club met in the Usual Resort last evening, the Reporter was besieged with questions as to the result of the glove fight between Santa Claus and his little daughter, which he had left the last meeting to attend, in the capacity of referee and time-keeper. He said that the fight had been to a finish; that there had been nothing in the way of a "draw" about. it, and that Kriss Kringle had been "bested" in great shape by his champion feather-weight. He not only threw up the sponge, but he added three jointed dolls, each with wax hair and real eyes; a wooden menagerie, headed by a rubber inebriate-asylum elephant that squeaked when compressed, innumerable picture-books, and countless toys besides. The jointed dolls, he said, fell early in the fray, and his humble little home now embraced within its walls all the awful horrors of the dissecting-room, with limbs scattered everywhere. Only yesterday, the progress of his foot into his shoe had been retarded by the presence therein of a *papier-mache* tibia and a card-board fibia, and as he left home there was a clinic being conducted on the remains of the last doll. Since the advent of the picture-books, the Reporter said, he had been engaged in poring over pages indented by such great truths as " This Is a Cat," and " Here We Have a Dog," and other revelations of natural history from which the opaqueness had been removed for the benefit of childish eyes and ears.  After offering his usual reward for any man who would not wish to be a father, the Reporter was suppressed, and the meeting allowed to proceed.

*  *
*

"Young Ned Sothern is here this week, and I think he is great," said the Actor.  "He is a very handsome fellow, and, as a consequence, he is greatly afflicted by that dreadful bane of fine-looking actors, yclept the 'mash note' in the profession.  But he pays no attention to these amatory screeds.  While playing the 'Highest Bidder,' in Montreal, recently, he made quite an impression on a young society belle, and she mailed him daily a quantity of angular handwriting on monogrammed note-paper.  Her feminine chums knew her secret, and, much to her chagrin, she was unable to exhibit anything in the nature of aftermath, as Sothern wasn't in the aftermath line.  Growing boldly desperate at his silence, she conceived a daring plan to meet him, and she made a wager with her friends that before he left the city she would spend a half-hour in his immediate presence.  In the auction-room scene of the 'Highest Bidder' there is a piece of marble statuary exhibited among the odds and ends there, and this venturesome damsel, who had noticed it, attired herself in drapery, whitened her face, and bribed the stage-door keeper and the property-man heavily to put her upon the statue's pedestal.  When the curtain went up on the scene, the girl's pose was perfect. Sothern came upon the stage and hung his hat on the projecting arm.  As he paused to soliloquize, his own arm inadvertently stole around the waist of the 'statue,' and immediately there was a chorus of 'Oh's' from a bevy of young ladies in a stage box. Sothern saw through the transparent trick in a moment; but he made no sign. Proceeding with the lines of his part, he began absently to tap the 'statue's' knee with the metallic auctioneer's mallet which he carried in his hand. The taps were none too gentle, and the feminine box-party exclaimed, 'Good gracious!' The 'statue's' black eyes flashed fire, and she blurted out, 'You're a brute!' Then, gathering her scanty drapery about her, she jumped from the pedestal and made a hasty exit. Sothern tried the real statue again the next night, but its presence in the scene gave him a cold chill, and he had it banished."

\* \*
\*

"I ran against that new automatic cigar gag of Kohl & Middleton's, the other day," chipped in the Agent. "It's a great scheme. If you desire an automatic and aristocratic cigar, you drop a dime in the slot and hold your hand under the box. Out falls the torch instanter. Then if you desire a *canaille* cigar, you insert a nickel, and when the result of the drawing is announced, you find yourself in a position to estrange your friends by igniting the vegetable. Ned Kohl says he is working on several improvements, and in a few weeks he expects to have the machine so perfected that it will give the base-ball scores in summer and remarks on the weather in winter. In the revised edition, Canadian coins or pant-buttons will not be legal tender. Kohl's partner, George Middleton, is seeking an inventor of an automatic bar, on which a man could lay down his change, press a button, and be served with a drink and an Arabian breath. I'm going to introduce him to a friend of mine who called on his family physician, the other day, and questioned him about his severe sore throat. The doctor examined him, and then informed him that his only salvation was whiskers or beard. My friend thought he said 'whiskey and beer,' and he has been full ever since."

*<br>\*

"Seeing Frank Lane here the other day," put in the Manager, "reminded me of the experience he once had in the company of John McCullough, the tragedian. He and Will McConnell were playing the entire mob in small town, and Frank's father, who was playing in the company, objected strongly to any stage foolishness in the way of 'guying.' One night, Lane the elder was playing *Icilius* in 'Virginius,' and the town where they were was Quincy, Ill. Frank and Will had found the Quincy beer very good during the afternoon, and when they showed up at the evening performance they felt remarkably well, and made an exceedingly vociferous mob. When the elder Lane came to rebuke the duet mob he spoke the line, 'Who uttered that evil word?' and his dutiful son answered, 'McConnell!' This greatly incensed the parent, and under his breath he muttered, 'Shut up, you loafer!' Then, proceeding, he inquired, 'Who uttered that evil word, I say?' and again Frank responded, 'McConnell!' The father was then choking with anger, and had to leave the stage, while McCullough stood in the entrance and heartily enjoyed the episode."

*<br>\*

"I desire," said the Purveyor, as he passed a damp towel over a moist section of his mahogany, "to file a protest here in open meeting against the Agent. He has done me up in great shape during the past week. Last Saturday morning he dropped in and told me that he had been appointed on the committee to watch Washington Irving Bishop, the mind-reader, in the afternoon. Bishop, he said, was to give the members of the committee a scarf-pin to hide within a mile of the Palmer House. Then he was to be blindfolded and find it. The Agent suggested that if he could arrange to hide it here, a big crowd would follow Bishop, and we would consequently have a big bar trade. As this proposition looked like business, I cheerfully agreed, and I went to work and cut up two dozen lemons as a starter. About five o'clock, in came the Agent and three other guys. One of them had a bag over his head, and the others were tied to him with strings. I had planted the scarf-pin behind the olive dish over there, and the guy with the bag on his head steered right for it, and found it. The gang which had followed them in set up a howl, and the Agent told me that the experiment had been a success of the first magnitude, and that I should set up the drinks as a starter. Well, I did so, and the round was worth at least two dollars, and when the gang had used it up, they proceeded to float out. Then, and only then, it was I discovered the guy with the bag on his head was the Agent's partner, and that a job had been put up on me. I now demand that the Agent be expelled from the Club, or be compelled to pay for the round. If this is not done, you can consider my resignation handed in." But rather than have such an important functionary resign, 'the Manager kindly discharged the Agent's indebtedness, and peace was once more restored.

* *
*

"This Inter-State Commerce Bill is pretty certain to knock out a number of our theatrical friends," remarked the Counsellor. "I have studied it, and I know whereof I speak. Those pale and thoughtful young men who invariably go down to the front-row seats to seek familiar

faces in each recurring comic opera chorus, will ofttimes
be disappointed in their quest, because each chorus fairy
will represent one full and well-developed railroad fare,
no matter if she is away in the back row.   There isn't
one of them who is able to ride on a child's ticket, you
know.   But, as the old saying is, 'it's an ill wind that
nobody blows in,' and it will lend a great impetus to the
local chorus-girl industry.   Big companies can not afford
to pay full railroad fares for members of chorus and
ballet, and, as a consequence, they will be obliged to
depend, in a great measure, upon our own home chorus-
girls.   To use a pastry expression, it will be 'pie' for
them; and when the young Chicago orchids, in full-
dress suits, wait at the various stage-doors after the performances, they will have the more satisfactory prospect
of purchasing beer and cheese sandwiches for home
talent; and all of the local dudes will become disciples
of protection, instead of the chorus free-traders, which
they have been in the past."

*  *
*

"The Agent's reference, awhile ago, to Ned Kohl, the
museum man," said the Night Clerk, "reminds me that
he was telling me, the other day, of a 'jay' who had a
funny experience here in town last week.   He arrived at
the Union Depot, and strolled up West Madison street,
in search of a quiet and comfortable hotel, where he
could economize.   Finally, he struck the Kellar House.
The hour was late, so he engaged a room, and lost no
time in retiring for the night.   In the morning he arose,
and found his way into the dining-room for breakfast.
Now you know that the Kellar House is the place where
all of the freaks put up.   The 'jay' was not aware of
this fact; consequently he was somewhat surprised when
he saw the pink-eyed Albino lady enter and make an

attack upon a large plate of wheat-cakes. Soon afterward, in came the living skeleton. The 'jay' began to grow nervous. Then the two Zulus ambled in, followed by the fat lady and the armless boy. This was too much entirely, and, with a yell of affright, the countryman bolted out of the building, and never stopped until he sank into the seat of the smoking-car on a homeward-bound train."

*.*

"Our friend Frank Lincoln, the funny man, often encounters some soul-stirring experiences while making the great American public laugh," remarked the Professor. "I refer to him as 'funny man' because I know he likes it. Sometimes he strikes a place where they wonder at him and his comedy more than they ever did at the old fifteen puzzle. Awhile ago, he was engaged to visit a suburban church, and entertain the congregation. He had been advertised as a 'monologue artist,' and so it was not known what he proposed to do. When he reached the church on the evening announced, he found a good house in attendance, and he was at once escorted up to the pulpit and given a seat next to the pastor. Pretty soon this pastor arose and offered prayer, asking a blessing upon the entertainment, after which he introduced Lincoln to the audience as a young man who would treat them to two hours of sanctified fun. This introduction made Frank feel as comical as a hearse-plume, but he pitched in nevertheless. Not a smile could he get, although some of the people present looked as though they would greatly like to unbend; and when he had finished, the reverend pastor arose, shook him warmly by the hand, and said: 'That was very good, Mr. Lincoln; but do you know, that once or twice I came very near laughing!' And yet there are people who think that life is one continued *charlotte-russe* to Lincoln.   He is expected to be real cute and cunning at all times and under all circumstances.   Even when out making a social call, he is never surprised in the least if his hostess says: 'Now, Mr. Lincoln, won't you please cut up for my little boy?'   Lincoln doesn't believe that there was ever any such place as Gilead, and I don't think you can blame him."

\* \*
\*

The Counsellor had been telling the Purveyor that he could easily perform the wonderful mind-reading feats of Washington Irving Bishop, but the Purveyor was just a bit shy on this point, having been victimized once before.   However, the Counsellor insisted; and to prove his rash statement, he allowed himself to be blind-folded tightly, after which he grabbed the Agent by the back of the neck and the apex of his pantaloons, and told him to think of something.   The ensuing silence was death-like and impressive.   Finally, the Counsellor reached into his upper vest-pocket, produced a cigar, and handed it over to the Agent.   That worthy accepted the weed, bit off its end, and lit it, at the same time declaring that the Counsellor had correctly divined his thoughts.   Then the other members insisted upon having their thoughts read, too, but the Counsellor refused to make any further tests, on the ground that he was broke; and the Club then adjourned.

"I have been out on the road this week," said the Agent, when the members of the Turnover Club had gathered in the Usual Resort last evening, "and I saw some evidences of show-life in one or two of the one-night stands which I was obliged to visit. These evidences were in the shape of show-bills. Of course you've all ridden through small towns and seen fragmentary mementoes of a departed circus pasted all over the corn-cribs. The balance of the fragments had gone to satisfy the cravings of the elements and the appetites of the local goats. In one town which I struck, I saw several very funny stands of bills, heralding shows that I never heard of before. There was the 'Original Double Mammoth Uncle Tom's Cabin Aggregation.' Why is it that all 'Uncle Tom' shows are 'original,' as well as 'double' and 'mammoth?' Can any of you tell? This particular show, through its advance agent, had ignited the dead-walls with some of the most lurid and incendiary wood-cuts I have ever seen. The poor blood-hounds represented were bigger than grain elevators, and were shown chasing a pale-green female, with a pink-and-white child in her arms, across a huge field of broken ecru ice, while following them up were several scarlet overseers and one or two dozen of assorted dark-brown colored men. The whole effect was very weird, as viewed by an unimpassioned bystander from across the public square."

\*\*\*

"Yes," put in the Actor, "I've witnessed many such sights during my career. To the lithographs displayed in the windows of country stores are attached slips of yellow paper giving the date of the coming show's appearance, and the admonition: 'Keep your eye on the day and date.' Many agents make this important line plainer to the 'jays' by inserting the lithograph of an eye. Then they usually put on another line informing the general public that there will be popular prices, and that seats are now on sale at the jewelry-store, opposite the post-office, and also at Gawkley's drug-store. Oh, yes, I've seen lots of 'em. The 'bus-drivers at the depots can tell an agent as soon as he jumps off a train. They all make a rush for him, and the one who finally secures him, asks him when his 'troupe' is coming—they invariably call it 'troupe.' Next, the landlord of the hotel informs him that his 'troupe won't do no business' if they haven't got a brass band; and if his show happens to be booked for a Saturday night, he is informed that he will surely lose money, because 'all the stores will be open' then. If the show happens to fall afoul of a church fair or a whist party, the show invariably gets the worst of it. One-night stands are great institutions, and the small town that is not able to boast of its 'opery house' is not in it at all. Never visit one of these places unless you have a brass band and your leading lady will consent to go out in the street parade, which is another necessity in a one-night stand."

"I was down at the Grand Opera House the other night," said the Agent, "and there I saw a new dodge which Charlie Williams, the treasurer, has introduced in the box-office. You know that ever since he and Ezra Kendall, the comedian, started out 'A Pair of Kids,' Charlie has been kept busy receiving telegrams about the business 'on the road,' and his pockets are always bulging with them. Finally, the messenger-boys at the telegraph office struck against so much work, and now the Western Union has run a wire and put an extra operator into the box-office of the Grand. Every night about seven o'clock, Charlie takes a seat near the instrument. It ticks out, and the operator reads: 'Oskaloosa, Iowa. The doors are open, and the police are beating back the eager crowds.' Charlie smiles, and lights a fresh cigar. More ticks, and: 'Money running out over the top of the box-office.' Then Charlie smiles twice, and lights two fresh cigars. Ticks again, and: 'Doors closed, and sign of no standing-room just put out.' At this, Charlie lights a whole box of fresh cigars. He declares that these are the messages from every town in which Kendall plays, and that he is thinking seriously of putting Manager Hamlin in the box-office next season, and running the Grand himself."

* *
*

"Our friend Bob Arthur is again with us, in the home of his childhood," said the Counsellor; "and again he is ahead of Herrmann, the wizard. Last week, Bob arrived in town, and at once sent a note to Arthur Cambridge, the dramatic agent, ordering the longest-necked actor he had in stock. In accordance with this order, Arthur surveyed his supply of histrions as they came in, one by one, to inquire for the letter that never came, and he finally picked out an artist with a neck long enough to taste a beer four times before it reached its destination. When this giraffe actor called on Bob, he was informed that he was wanted for Herrmann to behead nine times this week. The histrion said: 'If this is on the square, I wonder what my constituents in the one-night stands will say when they miss me.' But Bob disgorged a large silver dollar as a retaining-fee, and the contract was signed and sealed at once. 'I've got many an engagement on my nerve,' said the actor, as he affixed his shaky signature, 'but never before on my neck. I don't exactly fancy the job, but at the same time I have often awoke of a morning and wished someone would cut off the head I had from the night before.'"

\* \*
\*

"Horace McVicker was afraid he had a lawsuit on his hands the other day," remarked the Actor. "As he was standing in front of the theater, he was approached by a short, stout party, who glared at him fiercely, and asked if he was the manager. Horace thought he would chance it, so he said he was. 'Then, sir,' said the stout party, 'I want to inform you that, on that very windy day we had here last week, I was passing your theater, when a heavy iron rod from your banner up there fell to the sidewalk with a crash.' Horace looked the complainant over carefully, saw that he did not appear to be at all injured, and then silently awaited further developments. 'That might have killed me, sir,' said the man. 'How near were you to the bar when it fell?' inquired Horace. 'I was across the street; but had I been over here, I would have been in danger of sustaining great bodily harm,' was the response. Horace scratched his forefinger on his bronze mustache, and said: 'My friend, you don't know your luck. You were over there when this little iron bar of ours fell; but over where you were they have a long, mahogany bar, with looking-glasses and men in white aprons around it. Think what might have been the fearful result had that fallen on you! Make your complaint over there—we have all we can do to shinny on our own side.' The stout party went off scratching his head."

*<br>*<br>

"Our old friend Joe Polk, and his manager, Frank Cotter, have been with us all the week with their play, 'Mixed Pickles.' When they came here a year ago with it," said the Agent, "Frank went to a big pickle-house and contracted for a great quantity of small jars of mixed pickles to advertise his attraction. These he distributed free; and all of the retail grocers near the theater boycotted the show, because Frank spoiled their chow-chow trade by his singular method of advertising. But the play is very funny, and Polk is a very funny man. The other day, he was complaining a little of bad business, and there passed by a poor unfortunate whose two legs were off at the knees. 'What do *you* want to kick for, when you see such beings as that going about the streets?' queried the friend to whom he was complaining. 'I guess,' replied Joe, 'that I can kick a good sight more effectually than a man who has no legs at all!'"

*<br>*<br>

"Have you heard of the illness of Charlie Andrews' donkey?" queried the Manager. "Well, you know that this same little donkey is by all odds the best actor in Charlie's 'Michael Strogoff' company, and his sudden death would be a great blow to the organization. Andrews has called in the best medical skill obtainable in the veterinary line here, and has formally applied for relief to the Actors' Fund of America. To do this latter,

10

he has, himself, purchased all of the necessary red tape, at his own expense.  He declares that if this actor dies, he will have him stuffed, and carry him around the country, anyway.  Charlie seems to have remarkably hard luck with animals.  In the good old days here, he got a little gay one summer, and undertook to start out a 'Wild West Show'—and it was wild, and weird, too. Charlie went out West and purchased a live buffalo, paying $100 for it, and agreeing to pay $100 more upon its delivery here.  It arrived in Chicago shortly afterward, and Charlie paid the balance and the heavy express charges, before he found the buffalo was dead.  Then he invested in a pair of elks which were broken to harness, and undertook to drive them in the street parade; but, in the first block, they ran clear through the bass-drum in the band, and chased the scared drum-major to Washington Heights."

*\*\*

" Speaking about unruly objects in the show business," said the Actor, " reminds me of my recent visit to the People's Theater, with Manager Will McConnell, on the occasion of the opening performance of his new attraction—E. T. Stetson, in ' Neck and Neck.'  Will and his partner were, of course, very nervous.  Will told me, in confidence, that the great features of the play were the railroad train and the execution.  At rehearsal, the railroad train had gone all right, and it had been his sad experience in the show business that whatever went all right at rehearsals went all wrong at performances; consequently he was decidedly nervous about his two great features.  Well, the play proceeded to the railroad scene, and the locomotive came out of the entrance all right; but when it reached the middle of the stage, it shied and went right up the center aisle, shaking hands with the ushers, and never stopping until it had toppled over, and the Roman candle in the smoke-stack had bored a hole in the rear elevation of the orchestra leader's dress coat. Will was wild. He tore around behind the scenes, and when he returned, quite out of breath, he said that he had summarily discharged the engineer of the locomotive because he had not had his hand on the throttle. To cap the climax, the man who played the executioner, in the last act, was a little full, and he hooked the rope on the wrong noose, nearly killing the star. McConnell's hair turned gray that night. They closed the engagement last Saturday evening, and made the jump, with the scaffold and railroad train, to a store-house, without losing a night. This was because the cable-cars were held for Will after the performance."

\* \*
\*

"Your reference awhile ago to Horace McVicker," mused the Manager, as he turned toward the Actor, "reminds me that in the old days he tried to 'play-act;' and between you and me, he was a pretty queer actor. When Ned Thorne first came to the theater as the leading man of the stock company then playing there, Horace was essaying small parts. The morning after the first performance of the season, Ned strolled into the manager's office to inquire for his mail. Manager McVicker greeted him pleasantly, and asked him how he liked the company. 'I liked all the people except the young fellow who played the messenger—he is a duffer.' When Ned made this criticism, he noticed that Louis Sharpe hid his head behind the morning paper; and when, a few moments later, Mr. McVicker walked out, with a twinkle in his eye, Sharpe informed him that he had called the manager's son 'a duffer.' It was too good to keep, and it was not long before Horace heard of it.  The next week, the young actor was 'out of the bill;' and when Thorne strolled down under the stage one night, he found Horace with a long pole in his hand helping a lot of stage hands prod the canvas which represented the raging billows of the ocean upon the stage overhead.  Ned laughed at him.  'I'll get even with you,' he said to Ned, as he paused to wipe the perspiration from his reeking brow; and he did, a few days later.  Ned was a brother of the lamented Charles R. Thorne, Junior, and Horace introduced him to a friend as 'Mr. Thorne, a brother of the actor.'  Then Ned cried quits."

\* \*
\*

"Who is that young legal friend of yours?" asked the Actor of the Agent.  "I met him in here the other day, and he informed me that he was busily engaged in a criminal case.  Some days later I met him again, and inquired how his case had come out.  He said that his client had been discharged, but that he had not exactly been able to learn the reason why.  He said he had secured a pretty good jury, had made out a fair case, and had delivered what he considered a powerful argument, but the judge had instructed the jury dead against his client.  After the jury had been out about half an hour, he said they returned and wanted to know whether the prisoner had employed his own counsel or whether the court had appointed him.  The judge had informed them that the lawyer had been employed by the prisoner. When the jury came in again, your legal friend said, they acquitted the prisoner on the ground of insanity; and that is the point your friend could not understand."

The Purveyor here went down to the other end of the bar and shook dice with himself to determine who should close up, and the Club quietly filtered out through the side door.

# XVI.

In the temporary absence of the Proprietor, the regular meeting of the Turnover Club was called to order in the Usual Resort, last evening, by the Night Clerk. Just what he employed as a gavel is immaterial, and suffice it to say that, while some of its contents were spilled out, it answered the purpose admirably. While the minutes of the previous meeting were being read, it was noticed that the Manager was also absent; but he subsequently turned up during the call for unfinished business. How he managed to pass the cigar-stand without breaking the show-case will always remain a mystery, as his course from the front door to the telephone in the private office was very uncertain; but he finally landed in the vicinity of Mr. Edison's valuable patents, and grasped the receiver in a grip of iron. The effort of twirling the annunciator made him dizzy, but he found voice to call for the number he required, while the Club bravely held its collective breath, and awaited developments. "Hello! is that you, Maria?" queried the Manager, as he steadied himself against the safe. The response to this could not be heard, but the Manager said: "I'm here, dear, and I'm all right." The strain had been too much, and fairly before the last word had entered the transmitter, the Manager fell back with that traditional "dull thud" usually referred to in newspaper accounts of executions.   In the hurry and excitement of the moment, he neglected to release his death-grip upon the receiver, and the entire telephone accordingly forsook the wall and accompanied him to the floor, along with about fourteen yards of wire.   The members silently wondered whether the accompanying crash had leaked its sound over the wire to the ear of the anxious wife with whom he had been conversing.   They sorrowfully lifted him into a neighboring chair, and blocked his feet with a cuspidor, so that he could not slide off, while the Agent tried to replace the pieces of telephone with mucilage.

* *
*

"That girl at the central office just asked me if we were through," he said, as he dropped the remaining piece of the receiver, and rang off.   "Seems to me that when a man tears a telephone off the wall, he is pretty near through with it.   Wait until I ring up the coroner and notify him.   What's that?   Oh, well, if he's coming to, I'll stop a bit.   Guess he must have been out with wine agents to-day.   Speaking of wine agents, by the way, reminds me of a little experience of Harry Dixey, this week.   On Monday evening he discovered, in one of the boxes at the Chicago Opera House, an old friend of his, who represents a certain brand of champagne; and in the scene where *Dunstan Kirke* Howard tackles the turkey-lunch, Dixie said: 'You can't eat that lunch, old man, unless you buy a bottle of George Bouzet wine!'   Of course, the man in the box was agent for this particular brand, and was tickled to death over the compliment.   After the act, he took his friends out, and he purchased three quarts of Bouzet; and the following

day he sent a case of it to the comedian, with his best
wishes.   I was at the theater that night, and heard Dixey's wine gag, though I failed to catch the name of the
brand mentioned.   On Tuesday, I met three agents for
as many different brands of champagne, and I told each
one that Dixey had mentioned his particular brand in
'Adonis,' the night before.   They all sent Dixey cases
of wine, with their compliments.   The comedian hardly
knew what to make of this; but he finally decided
wisely, to make cocktails of it.   The agent of the
George Bouzet had 'a run for his money,' as it were;
but the agents of Ghouls Bums, Centerpole, and Sickoh
were all 'left at the post.'   Dixey now uses a bottle of
wine every night in 'Adonis,' instead of a pistol and a
pint of ginger ale."

* * *

"I met our old partner, Tony Denier, the retired
clown, the other day," remarked the Night Clerk.   "It
was up on Congress street, near his home; but I should
never have recognized him had he not been accompanied
by his famous bull-pup.   Tony was clad in a suit of
bill-poster's overalls, and there was a large slice of fresh
mortar imbedded in his écru whiskers.   I thought he was
a Knight of Labor, and should have passed him by had
not the bull-pup seized me by the pantaloons and called
my attention to them.   Then I asked him the occasion
for the disguise, and he told me that he had just performed the crowning act of his life.   You know he lives
directly across the street from the proposed big opera-
house and hotel—the Auditorium—and for weeks he has
been watching the work of excavation.   He knows the
contractor, and the other day he asked the privilege of
laying the first stone.   It was granted him, and he at
once rigged himself up as a real, live laboring-man, and

did the deed, of which he feels very proud. The men made the hole for him, and he attached the end of a crowbar to himself, and pried the big stone into it. Before he followed this up, by putting on the mortar for the second stone, he deposited in the hole a gaily-colored three-sheet poster of himself in his famous character of *Humpty Dumpty*, so that in after years it might bring up the past to the minds of John Blaisdell, Charlie Clayton, and other young men of the present day, who will doubtless be still doing business at the same old stands when the great building has crumbled into the dust. And then Tony went home to take the mortar out of his beard and paste it in his scrap-book."

\* \*
\*

"Say," broke in the Reporter, "I've written a 'pome,' and I'll read it to you. Here, don't run away! It's a short one, and it's a parody on 'The Blue and the Gray.' I call it 'The Jew and the Jay.' It was suggested to me by the Palmer House, where the Hebrews sojourn, and by the Sherman House, where the grangers put up. It's not long, and here goes :

### " THE JEW AND THE JAY.

*" With apologies to the author of ' The Blue and the Gray,' and with a dedication to Potter Palmer and J. Irving Pearce.*

" By the side of Chicago's river,
 Whence the fleets of lumber have fled;
Where the horrible odors quiver,
 Asleep are they all, in bed.

" Under the roof of the Palmer
 And the roof of the Sherman they stay:
Under the one, the Jew;
 Under the other, the Jay.

" Across from the County's building
 Is where rural transients go;

They blow out the gas and loan strangers ' stuff '
   When they visit the fat-stock show;
They leave their brogans in the hall-ways,
   They wonder at all the strange scenes,
And they drop the letters they've written home
   In the tops of the slot-machines.

      " Under the roof of the Sherman
        Is where all of this occurs—
          Where the man who is given a corner room
          Has his whiskers filled with burrs.

" Now let us look in at the Palmer.
    Can it be we have made a mistake ?
No, we have not, for there is Levi,
   And Izzy, and Ike, and Jake;
The rhinestones are there in abundance.
   Ah, me ! 'Tis a beautiful sight,
The rotunda is illuminated
   By electric and Israelite.

      " Under the roof of the Palmer
        The Hebrew travelers float,
        And the guests are awakened at two A. M.,
        By the colors in Joseph's coat.

            L'ENVOI.
    " So, under the roof of the Palmer
      And the roof of the Sherman they stay:
    Under the one, the Jew;
      Under the other, the Jay."

            * *
             *

"William Ananias McConnell is still with us," remarked the Actor, after the members had recovered,
" and I understand that he and Francis Murphy, the
temperance advocate, are to remain here some time.
It is now many moons since Willie donned the sock and
buskin, but he delights to relate the experiences he had
when he was an actor. He was telling me, the other
day, that he went out from Chicago once to play with

Harry Webber, in 'Nip and Tuck.' Will nipped, and Harry did the tucking. He remained with this company until the stage-manager made him dress with the donkey which the troupe carried. Will did not object to the leading man, but he drew the line at the donkey as a dressing-room companion. While McConnell was with the company, he did all in his power to make the life of the star miserable, but Webber bore it patiently, as Willie's big brother did his printing, and on that account he loved the family. One night in Peru, Ind., Will was playing the part of the doctor, and he changed one speech to the heroine by saying: 'You had better go into the house, my dear, for although this is Peru, it is chilly.' Strong men wept at this sally, and the laugh Will expected came not. After the performance, McConnell asked the landlord of the hotel why this little joke of his had failed to take. This landlord had visited the show on a trip-pass, and therefore didn't hesitate to give his opinion. 'My boy,' he said, 'every minstrel troupe that has been here for the last thirty-seven years has used that gag, and we saw it in Ayer's almanac of 1842 !' Will has been reading almanacs ever since that time."

\* \*
\*

"I was around to the James and Wainwright opening, the other night," said the Professor. "Gus Mortimer is their manager, you know, and he is a strong opponent of heavy lithographic and circus advertising. Between the acts he was arguing against this abuse to a lot of skeptics in the matter, and he declared it as his opinion that it did not help a legitimate attraction a particle to herald it in seven colors and a tint. At this, one of the skeptics sneeringly remarked that while the manager's statement may be true, it was nevertheless a fact that Mr. Mortimer was heavily billing his wife as a member of the James-Wainwright supporting company, and he thought this in very poor taste. Now, as Gus' wife was in the East, he was at a loss to understand what the man meant, and he asked him. 'You don't know what I mean?' was the reply. 'Why, don't you give a prominent line on your three-sheets to *Julie De Mortimer*, and isn't she your wife?' The burst of laughter which followed this rather staggered the fault-finder, and he closed up like a clam when he found that he had been making all this unnecessary fuss over Miss Wainwright's part in 'Richelieu.'"

*<sub>*</sub>*

"I see that Ned Kohl, of Kohl & Middleton, has at his museum this week the only living rival of 'Scully,'" put in the Agent. "Remember 'Scully,' don't you? I don't know whether 'Scully' is still walking or not, but I wouldn't be surprised to hear that he was. He was the champion pedestrian of his day, and he did his peregrinating in a South Clark-street saloon. I believe the track was about two hundred laps to the mile. When the saloon was deserted, Scully would sneak a little rest, despite the assertion of the big sign outside that 'Scully is still walking;' but when he would hear the click of the front-door latch, he would be up and off around his little tan-bark track, as though he had been at it all his life. I believe that he walked there for over a year, but the associations were too much for him, and in time it went from 'Scully is still walking' to 'Scully is a walking still.' I hear that this man of Kohl's—Snyder, of Indiana—could not quit walking if he wanted to. What a pie he would have had, had he resided over on the West Side during the street-car strike! He shaves while he walks, they say, but I'd like to see a barber follow him up and try to cut his hair. Tough job, that."

"I heard one the other day on our young friend 'Sam'l of Posen' Curtis," said the Reporter. "A week or so ago, his manager, Charlie Mendum, was approached in the Hoffman House bar, in New York, by several of the choice spirits technically known as 'the gang,' and informed by them that a running-horse had just been named after his star, M. B. Curtis, and that that afternoon the animal had won a race on the Guttenberg, N. J., track. At first, Charlie was loath to believe this, but he was assured that it was a fact. Then he hunted up · Curtis, and imparted the good news. The actor was delighted. He said it had always been the height of his ambition to have a race-horse named after him— especially a winning race-horse; so he opened several bottles of White Seal for the aforesaid 'gang.' After showing his appreciation of the honor in this manner, he started off for the pool-room to personally inspect the blackboard record of his namesake's victory. When he reached the place, one glance at the big board told the sad tale. Chalked up in great letters, and encircled by the winning ring, was the legend: 'Big Head, first.' Everyone appreciated the joke excepting 'M. B.' himself. He is rather touchy on the size of his cranium."

\*\*\*

The Agent had sneaked the Purveyor off to the farther end of the bar, and was indulging in a mysterious conversation with him. He wanted to borrow a dress-suit to wear at the opera. All he desired, in fact, was a dress-coat, as he believed he could turn in his dark vest, and hardly thought his plum-colored pants would show, in a box. Had he not gone too far, and endeavored to carry the idea that he was to sit in a box, he would have been all right; but at this, the Purveyor turned the sizzling seltzer-bottle full upon him, after which the members followed him out on to Clark street, and helped him to comb the seltzer icicles out of his whiskers.

# XVII.

"You will remember that we were speaking of one-night stand experiences at a recent meeting," said the Agent, as the members of the Club took their places in the Usual Resort last evening. "Well," he continued, " I was among the small towns this week, and I want to tell you about a troupe I ran across. It was a minstrel troupe, but I will not give you the name of it, as I am not yet tired of living. I chanced to be waiting at a small station, on the look-out for a train, which I subsequently learned was firmly anchored in a snow-drift somewhere up the road. The place I was at was a junction, and, about two A. M., a train on the cross-road toiled in, all covered with ice and snow, which told of a fierce battle with the elements. When this train stopped, it disgorged the troupe I speak of, which had played the evening before at a small town some twenty miles off. As the 'troupers' came into the station where I sat, they were a sorry-looking lot—cold, hungry, and travel-worn; but each man wore that unmistakable badge of minstrelsy, yclept a plug hat. These hats, in aggregation, might have served to illustrate the evolution of the modern silk tile from the much-abused accordeon. The specimen worn by the gentleman who carried the extremely large violin would represent the musical

11          (161)

instrument aforesaid, and through the troupe the form
and condition improved slightly, until the manager
appeared with a fairly good and presentable 'dicer.'

"These hats," the Agent went on, "all bore unmistakable evidences of a very severe winter, and they
formed by far the best portion of the troupe's attire,
considered as a whole.  Of course the manager's overcoat boasted of a fur collar and cuffs, but the fur had
deserted the hide in several places.  The distance of the
extremities of the troupe's trousers from the floor would
have aggregated many feet in the measurement—in fact,
if knee-breeches were in style, the members would have
had to sacrifice but very little cloth to be strictly *en règle*.
Large rents appeared in conspicuous portions of all the
garments, and there was a general air of dissolution
about the entire gang that was painful to contemplate.
They came in and hugged the stove with great fervor,
after piling up their scanty hand-baggage and battered
musical instruments in one corner of the waiting-room.
The manager went up to the station agent to inquire
about the train they desired to catch; and when he
informed his cohorts, a moment later, that there were
chances of their being obliged to remain where they were
all night, they said not a word in reply, but proceeded to
lie down upon the bare floor, around the stove, to seek
slumber.  One poor minstrel wore a pair of very sheer
trousers, and in his vain efforts to woo Morpheus he dis-
closed the additional sad fact that nothing intervened
between them and his bare legs—and the thermometer
outside twenty degrees below zero, at that.  Along about
daylight, this same young minstrel awoke from his fitful
slumber, and at once proceeded to wonder, in his artless,
burnt-cork way, whether 'the old man' would give them
a breakfast or not.  The 'old man' finally did gather

his forces, and trotted them over to the hotel, where he gave them a meal. For this they appeared truly grateful. The troupe was obliged to wait until eleven A. M. for a train, and it was my misfortune to be obliged to accompany them to the next town in the caboose of a way freight. In spite of all, they seemed a happy party, though. One over-worked plug of chewing-tobacco passed from hand to hand, also from hand to mouth, and a single copy of the *Clipper* was eagerly devoured in turn by those who could read. At the next town, they had to walk a very cold mile to another depot, to catch the train for the place they were to appear in that evening; and they could not pull their plug hats down over their ears, either. I tell you, boys, you know but little of show-life in one-night stands."

* * *

"Coming back from Detroit, the other day, I fell in with the Agent," remarked the Manager; "and it's mighty lucky we're here, as we had a smash-up on our way back. We had an end section in the sleeper, on the late train out of the Michigan town, and I slept on the main floor, while the Agent occupied the corner room upstairs. About one A. M., I was awakened from a sound slumber by a bump, and by muttered imprecations from above. It appeared that the air-brake hose from the engine had collapsed; and while we were standing still, a freight-train had endeavored to get ahead of us, and beat us into Chicago. But as there was only one track, this attempt was a dismal failure, and our sleeper had gone forward into the smoking compartment of the next car ahead, in an effort to get out of the freight's way. The Agent, who is always the rabid base-ball crank, stuck his head out of the upper room, and asked me whether I would call it a base-hit or an error. He declared, in

accents wild, that his head had been shot up against the
partition, and that the consequent bump on the top of it
was enlarging every moment.    Remembering the condition he was in, when he retired, I told him it was not
the bump that made his head large, and I advised him
to dress himself.    In a moment, he called down to me
that when he retired he had carefully folded up his pantaloons and placed them at the foot of his berth, but the
shock of the collision had put them on.    I was too
busily engaged in dressing myself to tell him how fiercely
I hated a liar.    Pretty soon we succeeded in getting out
of our battered car, via a sleeping-car ladder from the
rear platform, and surveyed the wreck from the vantage-
point of a Michigan prairie.    A few moments later, the
Agent tore wildly back into our sleeper, and came out
again with a huge bottle in his hand.    He supposed it
was full of reviving cocktails; but it was empty, and he
was obliged to content himself by chewing upon a piece
of lemon-peel he had saved from the wreck.    We went
forward into another sleeper then, and were soon sound
asleep, dreaming of our narrow escape, and rolling along
toward Chicago."

* *
*

"You know the Actor has a friend in the First Regi-
ment," put in the Reporter, "and he went out to the
Stock Yards the other day to call on him.    He's out there
defending property against the strikers.    Well, when the
Actor started for home again, someone yelled ' Scab!' and
in a minute there was a mob at the heels of the flying
innocent.    His mistake was in running at all; but once
started, he had to keep on, and he would have been badly
treated had not two officers rescued him, and conducted
him to the city limits.    Before he consented to allow
his preservers to leave him, he insisted upon purchasing

numberless beers; and when I discovered him, townward bound on a State-street car, he was busily engaged in gazing frantically at the company's posted rules, and trying to read them straight. After several vain efforts in this direction, he informed me that the rules were simply idiotic; and in support of this startling statement, he read one like this: ' Passengers will please not spit on the floor nor put their feet on the seats of the car except at the further crossing or in the middle of long blocks where sign is placed.' The Actor read this over twice, very painfully, and as the car was then directly in the middle of a long block, he expectorated in a vague, uncertain, and promiscuous manner. Such a rule, he declared, was the acme of idiocy. Pretty soon, the car paused at the crossing to allow a freight engineer to back up and start his train four times, and the Actor didn't know why the man next to him laughed out loud when he asked me: ' What's the matter ? Are they watering the horses?' Then he fell into a light doze as the grip-man caught the cable again. When he awoke, he said he felt ill; and he glared out of the window, and suggested that we go into ' that drug-store' there and get a bracer. I told him that 'that drug-store ' was composed of a row of red flannel lanterns on a dirt-heap along the track. After this break, he succumbed, and allowed me to inter him in his folding-bed."

\*\*\*

" The head which he doubtless was owner of the following morning, reminds me of the head Jack Saville once acquired through bad cigars," said the Professor. " Jack plays the genteel heavy part in Helen Dauvray's piece, ' One of Our Girls,' and in one of his scenes he comes on coolly puffing a cigar. Soon after he began to play the part, he went to Manager Hayden and told him that the cigars furnished him for this particular scene, by 'the property-man,' were fairly strangling him by their rankness, and he implored him to purchase for his use a box of at least three-for-a-quarter torches.   Jack became so importunate on this point that finally, in Boston, Manager Hayden promised to buy him a box of 'daisies.' Accordingly, he went to a friend of his, who is a cigar manufacturer, and had a special brand of cigars made. Saville lights the cigar just before he makes his entrance, and when he exits, a few moments later, he has consumed but about half an inch of it.   The special cigar which Hayden had made for Saville was composed of about three-quarters of an inch of the best Havana tobacco, while the rest was of a most appalling quality of the weed.   Saville heartily thanked his manager for the cigars, and he placed them in the bottom of his wardrobe trunk, beyond the reach of Joe Whiting, who dresses with him. 'Now this is something like, my boy,' he said to Joe that evening as he lit the 'fragrant Havana' tip of his cigar, and went on the stage.   After his exit, he carefully extinguished the torch, and filed it away in his 'make-up' box for future reference. At the close of the performance, he reproduced the weed, and relighted it for an enjoyable smoke on his way to the hotel.   Then it was that the plebeian body of the cigar began to get in its deadly work, and the awful fumes made the actor gasp for breath.   The next day, he related his peculiar and annoying experience to Manager Hayden, who informed him that the finest cigars were spoiled when once extinguished.   Until the entire box was used up, Saville consumed one of those tobacco *pousse cafés* every evening, and he never dropped."

* *
*

"I see that our friend Billy Crane, the comedian, is due here soon," said the Agent.   "Billy is a great epicure, you know, and his favorite dish is terrapin. Even his awful dyspepsia is forced to the wall when there is a dish of terrapin around. While he was playing in Newark, N. J., not long ago, his friend Ed Harris, the proprietor of the Genesee House, in Buffalo, sent the comedian a can of prepared terrapin with his compliments. Of course, Billy was delighted with the gift, and he spent the entire afternoon in sending waiters and bellboys to the cook's domain to tell him just how to heat the insect, and to warn him to add nothing to the dish but a glass of the very finest sherry. Then he invited a friend to dine with him, informing him of the delicacy to be anticipated, and when they entered the diningroom and were approached by a waiter, they joined in agreeing that terrapin was good enough for them, and they cared for nothing else. Pretty soon, back came the waiter, staggering under the weight of a two-gallon tureen of soup. The green hotel cook had taken the prepared terrapin and added water, butter, salt, and pepper. Crane tore his hair and pranced all over the diningroom in his anguish; but there was no terrapin. That night, after the performance, Billy dropped into the hotel bar for a night-cap, and found the porter serving out his terrapin soup as a midnight free lunch. This was the last straw, and the comedian threw up both hands. He never tried terrapin again in a queer hotel."

*<br>* *

"Of course it's a great scheme," the Purveyor was heard to say. He had been talking with the Agent on the quiet. "It's on the square, too, and you can just bet your sweet life there is really such a thing as the 'mind cure.' Now suppose, for instance, that you were possessed of a hallucination that you could get a drink here without settling for it with cash in advance. That would signify a diseased imagination in its worst stage. At this point, I bring my powerful mind to bear, in a strong effort to effect a cure. All this time, you firmly believe you will win the drink on credit. I think you won't. My mind is more powerful by several degrees than yours; hence I cure you of the hallucination completely. Savvy? That's the 'mind cure' you hear so much about. Now for another instance. You ducks think you want to remain here after twelve o'clock. I fix it in my mind that you can not, and I cure you completely and absolutely. See? We will now order a turnout. If you refuse to turn out, I think I can persuade the gas to do so;" and the Turnovers consented to turn out without further ado.          .

# XVIII.

When the members of the Turnover Club met, last evening, in the Usual Resort, the Agent and the Purveyor were found hatching another of their numerous Utopian schemes. The successful advent of the Japanese Village at the Columbia Theater had given the Agent the idea, and he held that there was great money in it. He proposed to organize and take over to Japan an American Village, in order to get good and even with the strange people of that far-off country, by giving them an exhibit of the arts and industries of this broad land. A Board of Trade friend of his had agreed to go along and sell puts and calls on wheat and corn. "This alone," said the Agent, "would make a big hit with the Japs." In a second booth, the Purveyor would dispense American mixed drinks; and in the third, there would be a covey of pool-sellers and book-makers. In one corner, an expert gentleman with a perspiration cloth would endeavor to make a collection of Japanese coins, with three cards and a shell game. Other well-known American arts and industries like these would make up the village, and the show would be heavily billed with United States three-sheet posters in four colors and a tint. The Agent said that he intended to go ahead of the show himself and make rates for the company at the Japanese hotels. His vast experience with divers and sundry " Mikado " companies had given him an insight into Japanese habits and customs, and he had no doubt that his own career in Japan would be the one crowning triumph of the American Village. His scheme was finally laid over for one week, because the members deemed it too weak.

\* \*
\*

"Our old friend, H. Waldo Johnson, or 'Hanky Panky,' will be in our midst again soon," said the Actor; "and if the stories I hear of him are true, it will be nec-essary that 'our midst' be of pretty good size, as they do say that his present girth is something enormous. This is the result of lolling life away at the seaside. He and Lou Weed, of the New York Casino, lolled it away together all last summer. 'Hanky' used to wear a straw hat with the rim chopped off, and a drooping 'Mikado' feather in the back of it, and he used to call himself 'Chief of the Laughing Water.' When asked why he had adopted this fanciful name, he would say, 'Because I laugh at water.' One bright day he went out shooting with a party of friends, and in his long rubber boots he deftly concealed several flasks which were not empty. When the party reached the happy hunting-grounds, 'Hanky' jumped into a boat, with his boots and breech-loader, and rowed out into mid-stream. From behind a clump of trees on the bank, his friends watched his movements. First, he tested each one of his flasks; then, he pulled up his gun and fired it aimlessly into space, and then he tested the flasks again. He continued wasting ammunition and testing flasks until his aim got so low that his friends feared he might add murder to his other crimes, and they sent one of their number to row out and tow him ashore. The next day he took a sail on Billy

Crane's yacht, and during the afternoon he acquired one
of his sullen fits.  The comedian vainly tried in every
way to cheer him up, and finally he appealed to his finer
feelings by asking: '"Hanky," will you have just one
drink with me?'  The portly agent pulled himself
together, gazed at his host a moment, and then solemnly
replied:  'I will, Bill, if I can't get two.'"

\* \*
\*

"Will Daboll, who recently played *Ravvy* in 'Erminie,' at Hooley's, claims to have been cursed by the
hardest luck of anyone on the road, this season," remarked
the Agent, who had come out of his Japanese trance.
"While in Cincinnati, he occupied a front room at the
hotel, and one night there was a big fire just across the
street.  The heat was intense, but the window in Daboll's
room was the only one on the hotel front that was broken
by it.  The weather was bitter cold, and the chill wind
played tag around the comedian's couch until morning.
The second day thereafter, Will was aroused at eight
A. M. by a loud noise out in the hall, and he jumped out of
bed and ran out to see what was the matter.  He discovered that the man occupying the room adjoining his
had blown out his brains, and this awful sight spoiled
his appetite for breakfast—at a high-priced hotel, too.
He resolved then and there never again to go out of his
room for the purpose of investigating mysterious noises,
for fear of losing a meal.  One night, soon afterward, he
found, before going on the stage, that there was a rip in
his coat.  He had some thread, and he went to every
member of the company to get a needle.  None could
be found, so he had to temporarily pin up the rent in his
garment.  When he went upon the stage, the first thing
he did was to run a needle into his foot.  Now what do
you think of that for hard luck?  Pretty tough, eh?"

"It doesn't always take an artist to make a hit," said the Professor. "When our old friend George Morris had his new melodrama, 'A Legal Wrong,' up at the People's Theater awhile ago, there was a hit made one night, but it wasn't made by a player. The cyclone scene in the play occupies the full stage. The wings are removed, and what is technically known as a 'sea cloth' takes their place. Its violent flapping raises all the dust on the stage. On this particular night, the scene had reached the point where a terrific storm is raging; everything is confusion; the hero is bending over the sinking vessel's bows, frantically striving to retain a salvation hold on his sweetheart, who has been washed overboard, and rescued by him; everybody's nerves are strained to the utmost in anxiety for the result. Just then, Mr. Morris, behind the scenes, directed the stage-boy to bring in water and sprinkle the dust down, as the ladies were choking. This boy was just making his début as stage errant that night. Not exactly grasping the situation, instead of sprinkling an invisible point, he walked deliberately out before the foot-lights, gazed around a full minute, and then began quietly spreading the water with one hand, as though he was watering cabbages. The house was full, and it took the audience a moment to wonder if it 'was in the programme' —then they broke out. It was the most tremendous applause I ever heard. Men got up on their seats and— yes, yelled. By the time the unfortunate boy had run the gauntlet of stage hands, he was completely broken up. They had to drop the curtain on the scene. When it was raised again, the audience renewed its applause, and cried, 'Bring out the boy!' and 'Trot forth the sprinkler!' That boy made the stroke of the season.'

"Speaking of unintentional hits," broke in the Actor, "I met an old friend of mine who—well, may be he's what you might call a 'fakir.' He's something of a magician, and in this capacity he sneaks out on the road with his wife once in awhile, and they raid the small towns. Of course, when they do this, there are but two in the 'company;' but you should see their printing! They used to call themselves 'The Gigantic American Silver Show,' and give away silver-plated nut-picks and diamond necklaces to their audiences—especially the nut-picks. The last time they went on an expedition, my friend told me they styled themselves 'The Mammoth World of Wonders,' and they advertised that every individual in the audience would be given a 'useful present.' One night they struck a tough mining-town, and they ran short of presents. They had been distributing pen-holders, slate-pencils, etc., when the supply gave out, and a riot seemed imminent. But my friend was equal to the occasion. He sent his wife out to sing 'When the Robins Nest Again,' and then he sneaked out via the back door, ran down to the post-office, and purchased a hundred postal-cards. These he distributed, on his return to the hall, claiming that they came under the head of 'useful presents;' and 'The World of Wonders' escaped from the town the following morning at daybreak."

* * *

"Something was said awhile ago about Billy Crane, the comedian," said the Agent. "He had a queer experience in Philadelphia recently, by the way, when he was playing there. The day after he opened, he received a beautifully written letter complimenting him upon his artistic performance of *Falstaff*. It was signed 'Your true friend.' Of course the comedian laughed over the epistle, as he receives many such. But the next day he received a second letter from this unknown admirer, in which he said that he had been sadly shocked by seeing him, after the performance, at the Continental Hotel bar, 'drinking with a roystering crowd of actors.'  Now this rather nettled Billy, but he said nothing about it.  On the following afternoon, he sat into a little poker-game with Mestayer and a group of choice spirits, and his surprise may be imagined when he received a third note from his 'true friend,' advising him not to squander, in such a profligate way, the money due his lawful wife. At this the comedian warmed up, and engaged detectives to trace the writer of the letters.  After his performance that evening, he visited a local variety theater to witness a glove-fight, and was made warmer the next day by another epistle, in which the mysterious correspondent expressed surprise that Mr. Crane should visit such brutal exhibitions.  These letters annoyed the comedian greatly. The only one he showed them to was his friend and brother comedian, Louis Harrison, who advised Crane to kill the writer on sight.  Two days later, came another letter upbraiding the comedian for 'discussing his epistles with an actor in a common bar-room.'  Crane finally left for Washington, without learning the name of his 'true friend,' and he never found it out until a Philadelphia paper came out with a two-column article about the affair, with copies of all the letters, which wound up like this: 'Comedian Crane doubtless is unaware of the fact that his "true friend" is none other than his old friend Comedian Louis Harrison.'  I'll bet Crane kills Harrison when he sees him."

* *
*

"Will McConnell returned from Indianapolis yesterday morning," put in the Professor; "and his visit to the Hoosier capital appeared to amuse him greatly.  One

night, while there, he went up the street to witness a conflagration, and he arrived at the scene before the fire-
engines came. Finally, one steamer rattled up, and the
firemen in charge of it dismounted, sat down upon the
curbstone in front of the burning building, and watched
the fierce tongues of flame lap it up. What? Yes, Mc-
Connell said 'tongues of flame.' After a time, Will grew
impatient at the delay, and asked one of the idle firemen
why they did not go to work and extinguish the blaze.
'You bet your life there's no jealousy in this department,'
was the reply. 'We don't go to work until all the rest of
the boys get here!' And Will declares that when 'the
rest of the boys' got there, there was nothing left of the
building excepting the cellar and a smudge. The day following, he was walking along the main street of the town
with a friend. The weather was very hot. A stranger ran
wildly by them in a mad chase after a receding street-
car. Said McConnell's Indianapolis friend, as he
mopped his brow: 'Just look at that —— fool running
for a car! I wonder if he doesn't know that there will
be another one along in ten minutes.' Will declares
that Indianapolis and her people are slower than their
time."

*.*

"I stopped in front of the Chicago Opera House yesterday afternoon, to take a look at the crowd of people
buying tickets for the Booth engagement," said the Manager, "when along came a seedy-looking chap, who looked
the people over, and dropped in at the tail end of the
line, with an expectant expression of countenance. As
he gradually neared the box-office window, he appeared
to grow worried, and he asked the man immediately in
front of him if he knew where the 'ticket peddlers' were.
The man informed him that he would find them soon

enough, and the seedy chap looked relieved at this. Pretty soon, he tapped his neighbor again, and pointing to a prominent citizen standing near the window, asked: ' Is that a republican or a democratic challenger ? ' The man questioned replied that he was a prohibitionist, he thought. ' That settles it,' said the seedy party. ' I thought this was a democratic primary, but if they're pro- hibitionists, I'll quit—there isn't a drink in sight; ' and he dropped sadly out of the line, with a sigh so deep that it chipped a piece off of the court-house cornice across the way."

* * *

For some minutes the Agent had been looking rather downcast, and when asked the reason, he said that he had been pondering over the action of a friend of his, who had proved himself the meanest man on earth. This friend had lost a brother recently, and had been given charge of the funeral. This brother had been born in Omaha, but had made St. Paul his home. His death occurred here in Chicago, and his brother did not know which place to take the remains to for interment. After thinking the matter over carefully, he had finally decided to take advantage of the cut-rates offered excur- sionists by the Burlington Road, and convey the remains to St. Paul, selling the return coupon for the corpse to a scalper there. After voting this thrifty friend of the Agent both the cake and the gate-money, the Club adjourned for one week.

Just as the members of the Turnover Club had left the
Usual Resort at the last meeting, the Purveyor started to
wind up his Waterbury watch, and when they dropped in
to attend the regular session last evening, he had just
finished the task, and was engaged in putting the time-
piece back in his pocket. He explained that he had but
recently purchased a new suit of clothes, and the Waterbury ticker had been presented to him at the same time,
as a sort of a chromo. Before he had finished winding
it the first time, he had worn out the clothes. Then he
had purchased a single member of a job-lot of pants, and
they bagged so dreadfully at the knees in two days' time
that it looked as though he was wearing woven-wire
bustles on his knee-caps. As a remedy for this disagreeable deformity, he had purchased, on the advice of
an alleged friend, a patent pantaloon-stretcher, warranted to reduce all swellings in the knees of pants.
Now this device had been constructed for able-bodied
trousers, and its effect on a pair of the genus job-lot
was bound to be disastrous; but the Purveyor did not
know this. Hence, when he awoke on the morning after
he had adjusted the stretcher to the job-lot trousers, as
per printed directions, he discovered, to his dismay, that
not only had the aggressive bagging at the knees been

removed, but that the knees in their entirety had disappeared, leaving a pair of knee-breeches in one vise of the patent stretcher, and a pair ot impromptu leggings clasped firmly in the other end. This parting had given him pain, he remarked to the Agent, and he offered a brand-new stretcher for sale on easy terms.

*<br>* *

" I heard one the other day that will bear repeating, I think," said the Agent. " It was on old Billy Birch, the minstrel man. It appears that he desired some legal advice in an important matter, and his partner in crime, little Charlie Reed, steered him against ' Eg' Jamieson, who attends to almost all of the professional law business in town. Well, Billy stated his case to ' Eg,' and received the desired advice from him. After the serious portion of the visit was over with, Billy started in to relate one of his famous funny stories, and in a moment the lawyer was all ears. In the adjoining room, there sat a very pretty young lady, who was hard at work manipulating a type-writer; and just as Birch arrived at the point of his narrative, this young girl's type-writer reached the end of a line, and the little warning-bell tapped, of course. At this, Birch looked at his friend in a sort of a discouraged way, and said: 'Come on, Charlie; let's get out of here. That's the second time this morning I've had that chestnut-bell sprung on me.' It required all of Jamieson's eloquence to explain to Birch that the bell attachment to the type-writer was a regular thing, and was in no way connected with the fabled chestnut-bell. Since that day, the bell has been muffled when clients were about."

*<br>* *

" I want to tell you all about the Proprietor's first experience with mixed drinks," said the Purveyor, as he

injected a modicum of Angostura bitters into the corner-
stone of a cocktail. "It happened over at the old place,
where we had the sideboard, this particular incident
did," he continued; "and one Sunday afternoon the
Assistant Purveyor appeared, to assume his watch, with
what we would term 'a very tidy load.' This disgusted
the Proprietor, and, with a very withering look, he bade
the man with the 'jag' go home for a 'snooze,' as he
termed it. Now you know that the Proprietor has had
but very little experience in the drink-mixing line, but
he anticipated a quiet Sunday afternoon, and he shut his
teeth firmly, in the resolve to force his patrons to take
straight whisky or nothing. Pretty soon, an absolute
stranger dropped in and coolly called for a cocktail. The
Proprietor looked at him fiercely, saw that he meant
business, and then went to work. He had often seen
me and my assistant mix a cocktail, so he proceeded to
squirt into a glass full of cracked ice a dash of everything he could find on the sideboard. He put in pepper-
mint, Angostura, Jamaica ginger, caracoa, absinthe,
benedictine, and, in fact, the entire repertory. The
stranger eyed him closely meantime, and when the
drink was handed over as completed, he took just a
suspicious sip of it, and then made a wry face. The Proprietor, who had been narrowly watching the effect of
his first effort upon its victim, said, at this sign of dis-
approval: 'Hold on, there! I guess I forgot to put in a
little lemon, my friend.' But the stranger pulled his
glass away from the outstretched hand, and replied:
'Never mind; you've got enough in here now to poison
me, and I don't want any more.' He finally downed it,
with an effort, but that was the first and last time the
Proprietor ever tried to mix a drink."

" I've got another drink-story that seems appropriate just now," said the Agent. " In the old Adelphi days, when poor Frank Clynes ran the refectory below stairs there, I dropped in one night, after the performance, and ran across Charlie Reynolds, the song-and-dance man, who had but recently returned from San Francisco. I sat down with him at a convenient table, and he proceeded to tell me of his experiences with earthquakes out on the coast. In the course of our chat, he went on to describe the feelings which overcame people upon the approach of the quake. The air grew awfully still, he said; a feeling of horror descended upon everyone, and conversation was carried on in awed whispers. One day these unmistakable earthquake symptoms developed, and Charlie said he looked for a soft place in which to fall. While on this solemn quest, he met a party of friends, and a drink was suggested. They all repaired to a neighboring drinkery, and just as the beverages disappeared beyond their respective palates, the dreaded shock came. One of the crowd, who had been inclosing numerous cocktails during the day, grabbed at the polished mahogany before him, steadied himself a moment, gazed vacantly at the barkeeper, and then asked, most seriously: ' My friend, what in thunder did you put in that drink of mine?'"

\* \*
\*

" There is a young actor in town this week who holds a good position in his profession now," said the Manager; "and I think he fully deserves his place, as he was made to serve a pretty hard apprenticeship. His tutor, by the way, was young Tony Denier, whose old father was well known as a pantomimist in the old days. The young actor in question was a member of a good family in a certain town where the pantomime company played.

He was badly stage-struck, and was possessed with a consuming desire to 'act out on the stage-boards.' With this feeling uppermost, he applied to young Tony, who was with the show, and he agreed to put him on the stage in proper shape. Accordingly, he was told to call at the theater that evening. He did so, and young Tony took him in charge. Steering him down to a dressing-room, he informed him that it would be necessary for him to black up in his first part; so he anointed him with lamp-black, and 'to make it more realistic,' covered him with it clear down to the waist. After this, the ambitious young man went upon the stage and cleverly enacted the rôle of a foot-ball for the entire company. In the last act, a rope was hitched to a belt about his waist, and he was drawn up to the 'borders.' He dangled there after the final curtain fell, as the stage-hands 'forgot' to loosen the rope. He was subsequently ordered to come down, in a stern, strong voice, by young Tony, as the latter came from his dressing-room some time later, and he sorrowfully expressed his inability to obey the summons. Then he was lowered to the stage, and he started to wash up, but the stubborn lamp-black resisted the onslaught of soap and water. Young Tony secured the fire-hose, and played a half-inch stream on the neophyte for awhile. When they got him under control, they sent him home, thinking him cured of his craze; but, when the troupe left town, the next morning, the ambitious young fellow was down at the station to see them off, his unconquerable soul filled with a consuming longing for the foot-lights, and his eyes and ears filled with the aforesaid affectionate lamp-black."

\*\*\*

"Speaking of ambitious histrions," said the Actor, "did you ever visit one of these dramatic agencies around town? There are several of them, and they have various brands of actors and actresses on draught at all hours. At any time, they can tap for a 'leading heavy' or a 'juvenile.' One of these agents showed me a letter the other day from an actress. Here it is: 'North Judson, Ind., June 6, 188—. Mr. ——. Kind sir:—What I want to know is this, have you any opening for a *good* general biz Lady. I will be at liberty after Satderday. we Close here. Know I dont want Just anything Just so i get a chance to act. I want some thing I can get my salary. Thats what im after. will work prettie cheap for Summer Season. dont want any thing like you got for Mrs. ——, *The Gem*. Mayby you have herd her speak of me. can do (or do at) moast any thing. *have no* photo to send. aint you sorrie for that. answer soon and let me know how mutch dependance I can putt in you. very respectfuley yours, —— ——.' How's that for an application?"

\*\*\*

"Here is another curiosity in the same line," said the Agent, "and I'll read it just as it is written. Here goes: 'Philadelphia july 10th 188—. Dear sir i hope you will excuse me for useing your time but as i seen your advertisement in the new york Clipper i take up my pen to answer one of them i am a young man 19 years old 5 feet 9 inches high. weight 143 pounds in the best of health always. well built solid and possess a remarkably strong and stern voice and can take it down low and easy at times i got good actions can imitate all the leading actors that come to this city such Mr Oliver D Byron james O'neill harry lacy Edmund collier Dominick murry Edwin Thorne john A stevens George Carock and in fact all that i have seen besides what other theaters i been to i go to the national every week while it is open i have

acted there two week and great applause and was offered
a job with a company but my mother took sick just then
and I had to throw up the job besides acting at the
national I have acted in Philadelphia about 20 Different
places in all the concerts halls and places of amusement
there is here i can play either a leading role villian or
detective i am endorsed all my friends and all who seen
me act and i would have manager and proprietor of the
national signed here if i knew where they lived.  i have
know more to say just now but when you. hoping that
you will address your for Me —— ——, —— st Phila
Pa.'  Now what about that ?  Isn't it a corker ? "

*\*\*

" I see that Charlie Foster has had his three bull-dogs
photographed," remarked the Night Clerk.  "Roe, of
Robinson & Roe, performed the operation, and the dogs
were supported by their owner and by young Frank
Moynihan, who has gained much fame by his stage por-
traitures of Irish policemen—in fact, he is termed 'the
only Irish policeman on the American stage to-day.'  Mr.
Roe, you know, is rather a nervous man, and he eyed the
trio of bull-dogs suspiciously before he began.    Well,
Charlie and Frank posed the three of them on a set rock
at the farther end of the gallery, while Roe proceeded to
draw a bead on the group with his camera.  When all was
ready, he warned his two amateur assistants not to med-
dle with the dogs, and then he asked Charlie their names.
Obtaining the information, he seized the trigger of the
camera, and cried: 'Tip ! Bob ! Nell ! Rats ! ! '  This was
for the purpose of making the dogs prick up their respective ears and appear on the alert in the negative, but the
effect of it was electrical; the dogs bounded from the set
rock in all directions, and Mr. Roe left the gallery by the
new instantaneous process and a side door.  Pretty soon,

he cautiously reinserted his head, and timidly inquired: 'Will they bite?' For a few moments after the first alarm, the place was full of dog, and camera, and set rock. Moynihan indulged in a fit, while Foster rounded up his livestock. Then Mr. Roe finished the operation, wearing a catcher's mask and carrying a lawn-tennis bat the while. He said it would not be at all necessary to bring the dogs around to see the proofs, and declared that he would much rather take a group of chorus-singers or a dose of castor-oil than a trio of fierce bull-dogs who appeared to consider the word 'Rats' a personal affront."

\*\*\*

Just here, the glasses behind the bar began to rattle violently, and the building shook beneath the feet of the Club. The gas flickered, and the clock lost four minutes. Visions of a Charleston visitation arose before Turnover eyes, and the frightened Agent was at once dispatched to ascertain the cause of the terrifying upheaval. He soon returned with the information that the extremely large and fleshy colored woman on exhibition over at Kohl & Middleton's Museum had coughed. Taking warning by this, the members all indulged freely in cough-syrup, and then adjourned.

SOAP IN A COCKTAIL—The Purveyor's Understudy Attempts to
  Shave the Ice—A Bad Break—Edwin Booth Shot At—Jimmy
  Devlin as Call-Boy—Will McConnell's Abscess—Major Benton's
  Minstrel Troupe—Doc Trimen's Ball Match—Harry Pitt as an
  Umpire—Harold Fosberg's Acting—Dynamite!

When the members of the Turnover Club dropped in
at the Usual Resort last evening, to attend the regular
weekly meeting, the Purveyor and the Agent were found
engaged in a serious dispute. The latter declared
that the cocktail which he had just disposed of tasted
strongly of castile-soap, and against this he entered a
very strong protest. The Purveyor explained the matter by saying that in the morning he had attempted to
initiate a new "understudy," and he had first instructed
him to go down-stairs in the cellar and shave the ice for
the day's mixed drinks. As he was an unusually long
time at the task, the Purveyor said he went down into
the hold of the bar-room to see what was up, and there
he found the promising young understudy, armed with a
brush, busily engaged in covering the cake of ice with a
thick lather preparatory to shaving it with an old razor
which he had in his hand. Right at this stage of the
proceedings, the Purveyor said, he had taken it upon
himself to give the new man his discharge papers, and
he had shaved the ice himself, in the regular, orthodox
way. Hence the taste of soap in the cocktail, which
could not be entirely eradicated, though he had noticed
that before he had filed his complaint the Agent had
entirely eradicated the cocktail in question. He sug-

gested that the Agent indite a testimonial to the soap
manufacturers, expressing his appreciation of their production. This, he said, was the only way in which he
could get even; but the Agent absolutely refused to give
his lithograph a chance to appear in any soap advertisement.

*\*\*

"The other day," put in the Actor, "I heard Frank
Moynihan and Jimmy Devlin talking about Mark Gray,
the crank who shot at Edwin Booth, in McVicker's
Theater, some years ago. Both of them were in the cast
of the piece which was being played that night. Frank
was then the regular call-boy of the theater, and he
appeared in small parts. In this play, which was 'Richard
II.,' he and Devlin were two of three desperadoes who
rushed in and fought the star with swords. While waiting for their cue to go on, they sat behind the 'flat' on
the steps of a stage throne. At the time, Booth was on
the stage alone, reciting a long speech. When the trio
heard the first shot, they supposed that the 'property-
man' had accidentally discharged a revolver. At the
sound of the second shot, Moynihan and Devlin rushed
around to the second entrance, and looked out on the
stage. Booth had by this time stepped forward to the
foot-lights, and was saying: 'Ladies and gentlemen, if
you will wait until I retire and assure my wife that I am
unhurt, I will resume my part.' He left the stage amid
a dead silence, went directly to the green-room, spoke
to his wife, and then came back to take up the thread
of the play again. After he had finished the performance
and was leaving the theater with Mrs. Booth, he learned
for the first time that he was the intended victim of the
shots. 'My God!' he exclaimed, 'was the man shooting
at me?' He supposed, all the time, that some drunken

man in the audience had been fooling with a pistol, and
had accidentally discharged it. When he learned the
truth, he went back on the stage, had the lights turned
up and the flats shoved on, and for the first time realized
his narrow escape from assassination when he found the
two bullets embedded in the wood-work of the scene.
Had they not struck the wood-work, they would have
killed Devlin, probably, as he was sitting directly back of
the ' flats.' "

\* \*
\*

" This same Jimmy Devlin used to be the call-boy at
McVicker's once," remarked the Manager, "and one
evening he was standing in the ' prompt entrance ' with a
prominent actress who was starring at the house then.
One of the members of the cast spoke the line, ' Do the
stars remember us ? ' whereupon Jimmy turned around
and said, dryly: ' That line was written for the call-boy.'
The actress appreciated his remark so highly that she
' remembered him ' with a five-dollar bill at the close of
the engagement. In those days of stock-companies and
traveling stars, by the way, the latter always signalized
his or her last night in the house by presenting the call-
boy, property-man, and stage-hands with little money presents in recognition of little services rendered during their
stay. Jefferson was always one of the most liberal stars in
this direction. Lotta always gave freely, and so did Billy
Florence, and they never lost anything by their generosity."

\* \*
\*

" Our old friend William Ajax McConnell has had
a new star on the road for about six weeks," said the
Reporter. " It is an abscess which a colored three-sheet
poster could not begin to do justice to, and it is located
in his jaw-bone, just abaft the left ear. Will says he has
exploded the old sentiment to the effect that ' abscess

makes the heart grow fonder.' After he had thoroughly
exploded it, a large and able-bodied physician came to
the bat, and proceeded to explode the abscess. He said
that he had used a lancet in the operation, but Will says
that when he was a boy they called it a pickax. The
abscess, when it was in perihelion, drew his entire attention around to one side of his face, and he was obliged
to smoke siphon cigars, for which he could borrow a
light without turning his head. When he had fully made
up his mind to die, he used to sit at the window and
watch funerals go by, and he declares that at least forty
funerals per day passed down Wabash avenue. He says
he thought there must be a cholera epidemic out in
Englewood. Of course he could eat nothing, so he read
the Dorcas Society Cook-Book three times a day, and
took his medicine before each meal. He has been
stopping up with his brother John, manager of the
Columbia, and during his illness, he has run the whole
gamut of John's book-case, eagerly devouring everything
in sight in the literary line, from a copy of Young's
Night Thoughts to an almanac of the vintage of '69.
At the time when his star, the abscess, was drawing the
largest houses—when the simple fluttering of a window-
curtain was like a stab with an auger to him—John's
litle girl used to playfully climb up on the head-board of
Will's bed and balance herself just above his pet.
Finally, the sufferer secreted a newspaper filled with coal
under the sheets, and when his little visitor appeared at
his door he would threaten to heave large gobs of
anthracite at her if she tried to steal second-base on him.
Oh, Will has had large amounts of pleasure!"

\* \* \*

"Major Benton, who was formerly with the Columbia,
is still in town," put in the Night Clerk, "and he says

he thinks he will have to have the Inter-State Commerce Bill repealed. It was bad enough, he declares, to be obliged to hustle along with a company when the old latitude in the way of rates was allowed, but it was almost certain death to a show nowadays. He was telling me that at one stage of his professional career he managed Arnold's Minstrels, in which there were thirty artists, each one of whom wore a gold-braided cap with the name 'Arnold' across the front. Late one night, they left Rochester to go to Syracuse, and before they boarded the train, Manager Benton, assembled his cohorts, and informed them that, owing to a slight discrepancy in the box-office receipts, he had been able to purchase but twenty-three railroad tickets, whereupon his loyal forces agreed to help him out. It was a very long train, and when the conductor started to go through it, after it had pulled out of Rochester, he found Benton in the front seat of the forward smoker. He handed over the bundle of tickets with the remark that he could not miss his people, as they all wore the Arnold caps. In about half an hour the bewildered conductor came back to Benton and said: 'Look here, my friend, if there is one of those —— caps on this train there a thousand of them?' But Benton protested that there were but twenty-three of them. The 'Pompeys' had followed, passed and repassed the conductor on his way through the train, and several traveling men had 'caught on' and borrowed the caps to wear. When the conductor started through a second time, the manager glanced out of the front window and saw three of his end men and the clarionet player sitting out in the cold, on the steps of the baggage-car, trying to look pleasant. When the mystified conductor had finished his third trip without result, the engineer whistled for Syracuse, and the troupe escaped unhurt."

"One of the greatest base-ball cranks in town is 'Doc' Trimen, the druggist," said the Reporter, "and it is seldom that he misses a game. Of course, he took in the recent struggles with the Detroits; and at the final contest he was accompanied by a friend who knew nothing whatever of the sport; so the 'Doc' proceeded to explain the points to him. I suppose you have sometimes attended a ball-game, and sat near a man who was having the rules explained to him. It's pleasant. Well, on this occasion, the 'Doc' was an excellent tutor. 'There,' he said, extending his finger toward 'Old Ans,' 'are the bases, and that square is the home-plate. Those white lines are the foul lines. When a batted ball goes this side of them, it is foul; and, if it goes on that side of them, it is fair.' Just at this juncture, 'Malaria' Thompson, who was at the bat, struck a terrific liner, which struck the 'Doc's' pupil right bang in the eye, and knocked him senseless. Restoratives were immediately applied, and the people crowded around the unfortunate man to give him air. The 'Doc' took his poor friend's head in his lap, and bathed it prodigally. Finally, the efforts were rewarded, and the man opened his eyes and gazed about him in a dazed, Panorama-place manner. At last he caught the 'Doc's' reassuring look, and feebly inquired: 'What was it?' Always thinking of the game, the 'Doc' replied: 'It was a foul.' His poor friend closed his eyes wearily, and murmured: 'Oh, I thought it was a mule!'"

\*\*\*

"Your speaking of base-ball," remarked the Agent, "reminds me of a good one told me the other day by Frank Lane, of Agnes Herndon's company. It was on Harry Pitt, the English actor—that is, he was born in this country, but he is awfully English, you know. Well, he was asked one day, in New York, to umpire a game of base-ball. He didn't know much about it, but in the goodness of his heart he consented to officiate. The first man at the bat made a beautiful base-hit, and took first bag. The next man hit a vicious liner over third base, and the third-baseman jumped high into the air and pulled it down with one hand. Then, to make a double play, he slammed it over to first base. The first-baseman caught the ball just as the runner slid back to the bag. It was a very close decision, and the guardian of first base shot out one hand in an appealing gesture toward the umpire, and shouted: 'How's that?' Pitt recovered himself sufficiently to ejaculate, admiringly: 'Bloody wonderful, my boy!'"

\* \*
\*

"When Miss Herndon was playing over at the Standard," put in the Actor, "Lane stopped at the Farwell House, and Harold Fosberg, of the 'Beacon Lights' company, then playing at the Academy, also stopped there. Harold, you know, is a great character, and is always acting, whether on the stage or off. Poor Charlie Thorne was his idol, and he was always imitating him. Well, one matinee day, Lane came out from dinner with him, and Harold hailed a Blue Island avenue car. 'You don't mean to tell me that you ride those two blocks, do you?' queried Frank. The car had stopped at the crossing, and Harold swung himself onto the back platform. As he did so, he turned, and, with a theatrical wave of his hand, tapped his breast and said, melo-dramatically: 'Poverty should walk! My heart so light, and Paris so gay!' The conductor thought he was a crank, and the passengers seconded the motion."

"Dynamite!" yelled the Agent, as an explosion
occurred; but the excitement soon subsided. It appeared that the Reporter was about to start for home,
and desired to ameliorate his pungent breath somewhat;
so he burrowed in his vest-pocket for a cassia-bud. By
mistake, he secured the industrious end of a parlor-
match, and as his teeth closed upon it, the explosion
referred to occurred. His mouth was so blistered by it
that he was unable to tell the number of his residence,
and the Club put him on a homeward-bound car, with a
lump of ice on his tongue, and a breath like a gas-stove.

# XXI.

When the members of the Turnover Club met in the Usual Resort last evening, the Agent and the Purveyor had a new scheme on the broiler. The former was very anxious to put a company on the road during the summer months, and he had hit upon a new and brilliant idea. The troupe was to consist of the Purveyor, his understudy, and Bacchus and Ganymede, of the Order of Full Moons. The Agent was to go ahead of the show himself, and when he reached a desirable town, he would go to the leading rum palace in the place and make arrangements with its proprietor to play his combination for a week. Then he would proceed to flood the town with handbills, and when his aggregation arrived, it would follow this up by flooding the townspeople with mixed drinks. Each one of the quartet selected were past masters in the art of liquor-juggling, and their adroitness in this line would attract large crowds, while the Agent, as representative of the combination, would pocket fifty per cent. of the gross receipts. The troupe would carry no scenery, the audiences furnishing their own scenery to suit the taste after they had encompassed the repertoire of beverages. Each member of the combine would execute a solo or two at

**13**          (193)

each performance, Bacchus performing his specialty on the frozen punch without using a net or leaving the stain. By carefully avoiding the prohibition circuit, and giving a street parade every day, the Agent was of the opinion that this novel entertainment would be a go; and as an afterpiece, he proposed to have the full strength of the company in a pyrotechnic display of chemistry that would rival Professor Paine's " Destruction of Pompeii." The Actor sneered at the project when he learned that the Agent had decided not to pass the profession.

\*\*\*

" Early the other morning, just as I got off watch," remarked the Night Clerk, " I ran across a friend of mine who was on his way to one of those department stores to make some purchases. He bought some coffee, some matches, some tin-ware, had his photograph taken, and experienced an easy shave, all on one floor. The shave was given with the coffee. With tea, they throw in a dry shampoo. Well, as we were leaving the place, he insisted upon buying me something, and I finally selected a small dollar clock. The salesgirl wrapped it up, and I put it in my overcoat-pocket. It was ' warranted to go in any position,' and I think Captain Anson should lose no time in securing two of them—one for pitcher and the other for center-field. But how that little clock did tick ! People heard it on the street, and gazed critically at my clothes. Guess they thought it was a Waterbury. I had to go and see a man on business, and of course the clock had to accompany me. The man looked me over, and then inquired if the twelve apostles came out only one an hour, or oftener. Up to that time, I had not been aware that there was an alarm connected with the infernal little machine; but there was no mistake about it. The noise it made when it shot off was deafening. Every man in the building rushed to his telephone and yelled, 'Hello, Central!' I fired the awful thing down into the street, and an expressman nearly fell from his wagon in a wild attempt to get out of the way of what he thought was the fire-insurance patrol. A policeman turned in an alarm, and all was excitement. Finally, the officer found the clock, broke it open with a rock, and took from it a spring long enough to officiate as a loop cable on the State street line. If you want to spend a dollar and get your money's worth, just buy one of those dollar clocks."

\* \*
\*

"Little Willie McConnell is with us again," said the Agent. "He returned last week, and his friend Tony Denier killed a *papier-maché* fatted calf in honor of the occasion. I met Willie yesterday, and was amazed to find his face all covered with scratches. It looked, with its bars and dots, like a libretto of S. G. Pratt's 'Lucille,' and I asked him what it meant. He informed me that, in an evil moment, his brother John, manager of the Columbia, had invited him to his house the night before to stay all night. Will accepted the invitation, and, when he was quite ready to retire, he was shown to the folding-bed in the front parlor. Before leaving him, John brought an alarm-clock, and informed Will that he had arranged it so it would explode at 8.30 A. M. Then Will went to bed. The clock began work precisely at midnight, and fought a round every hour until morning, when the works finally knocked it out. Along about daylight, John's pet cat strolled into the parlor, and jumped upon the folding-bed. After Will had become convinced that it was a real cat, he allowed it to lie down beside him and slumber. John came in about nine o'clock.

He is a little near-sighted, and, as Will and the cat were concealed beneath the cover, he supposed the bed was empty, so he at once threw it into an upright position. When Will came to, he found himself standing upon his head on a pillow, and the pet cat making wild struggles to release himself through his face. Will's frantic cries for help attracted the neighbors, also the patrol wagon, and a blacksmith separated him and the scared cat from the bed. That accounts for the furrows on his open countenance."

* *
*

"Nat Goodwin is catching on in New York City in his new burlesque, 'Little Jack Sheppard,'" put in the Actor. "His manager is 'Hurricane George' Floyd, who writes one of his peculiar, 'razzle-dazzle' letters to me to tell of the success of the red-headed comique. Nat's latest yarn is a good one. You know his favorite tales are those relating to the pleasures and vicissitudes of the fascinating game of draw-poker, and this is one of them. It is about a stranger who was roped into a poker game by a card-sharp. After playing along awhile without incident, the sharp proceeded to insert his fine work, and he dealt the stranger a big hand, giving himself a larger one. As the stranger skinned his cards, a look of deep suspicion stole over his countenance, and he carefully proceeded to inspect the backs of his cards. 'These cards are marked,' he declared, finally. 'Nonsense,' replied the sharp. 'Yes, they are pricked with a pin,' protested the stranger. 'You're foolish,' said the sharp; 'those are only fly-specks.' The stranger reached for the rest of the pack, and looked them over closely, while the sharp twitched uneasily in his chair. Finally, the stranger looked across the table, and exclaimed: 'Fly-specks! Pretty high-toned flies to pay attention to nothing but aces and kings.' And the card-sharp threw up both hands."

*<br>*  *

"The other day," said the Reporter, "I went into a wholesale music store over here, and while I sat waiting for the man I had called to see, I heard a stock-clerk and the shipping-clerk fill a country order. It sounded very funny to me. 'Thirteen White Wings,' yelled the stock-clerk, and 'Check,' responded the shipping-clerk. Then they started in in earnest, like this: 'Four Robins Nest—Check; six Stick to Mother—Check; nine Starry Eyes—Check; two Peek-a-Boo—Check;' and so on, *ad lib.* Do you notice my musical terms, by the way? The only musical terms they use in that particular establishment, however, are.'Cash,' I understand."

*<br>*  *

"Speaking of popular songs," said the Manager, "reminds me of a good one on Charlie Reed and Billy Birch, of the Chicago Minstrels, which occurred the other day. It was last Saturday, and after the matinee they went out for a stroll together. The day was so fine that time slipped by unheeded, and they realized only too soon that they barely had time to get back to the theater to black up for the evening performance. Charlie suggested that they drop into a restaurant and snatch a bite, but Billy said he was afraid that the proprietor might be looking. However, they finally entered a 'mealery' where they give a song and dance, an oratorio, or a pathetic ballad with every fifteen-cent meal, instead of a piece of pie. Charlie called for a quick oyster stew, and when the order was placed before him, a young lady in evening dress mounted a platform at the end of the room, and a young man began to chase his fingers along the foreground of the piano-forte. Just as

Charlie struck his first oyster, the young lady began to warble 'Peek-a-Boo' to the young man's accompaniment. This was pretty good, so Birch ceased chewing Reed's cabbage and gave his own order. 'One batter-cakes and coffee; When the Robins Nest Again!' yelled the waiter, in stentorian tones, and the young lady started in on this ballad as Birch's order arrived. Charlie reached for his trusty chestnut-bell, but found that he had left it on the other vest. This, Birch said, when he offered the excuse, was a canard to make people believe that he owned two vests. A stranger came into the place, took a seat at the next table, and gave his order. 'Half on the shell, and White Wings!' and the songstress drifted dreamily into this ballad as the stranger tried to squeeze a dry lemon onto an alleged blue-point. And this was the way it went: 'Lottie Lee' accompanied a small steak, 'The Bould McIntyres' went with potato salad, and 'Only a Pansy Blossom' with poached eggs. Charlie and Billy thought that the idea of giving a free concert with every stew was indeed a great one, and Charlie has already written to 'Frisco regarding the scheme."

*⁎*

"Your reference to the McConnell family awhile ago," said the Professor, "reminds me that Will, of that ilk, was quite a sporting man in the old days, and he was never happier than when he was acting as 'capper' for someone's game. He was telling me the other day about the time he traveled around the country with a chap who had a patent egg-tester for sale. The man didn't know much about the 'faking' business, and Will undertook to post him up. In the first place, Will had an egg boiled very hard, and gave it to the egg-tester man with explicit instructions as to its use. At the next town, a crowd was collected on the street-corner, and the egg-tester man addressed the people thuswise: 'Ladies and Gentlemen—You no doubt believe in the old idea that a person can tell whether an egg is fresh or not simply by looking through it endwise. For instance, you can not see through this egg,' holding up the hard-boiled one for inspection; 'yet if I place it in my egg-tester here, you can see through it clearly.' Here the egg-tester man substituted a raw fresh egg for the hard-boiled one, and carried out his promise. Then Will, in his capacity of 'capper,' came up and purchased one of the testers, and, as he says, the 'jays' followed suit, and a harvest of dollars was reaped. 'We should have been making money on the scheme yet,' said Will, 'if the chump hadn't got nervous one day and dropped the boiled egg. They drove him out of town.' "

* *
*

"I've got a good one to tell you on the Agent," put in the Actor. "He and I took in the Exposition together the other day, and while up in the gallery we ran across the booth of a phrenologist. The booth was temporarily in charge of a mild-eyed young man with a mildewed complexion, who called the attention of passers-by to an extensive phrenological chart on the counter before him. The chart represented a man's head, of abnormal size, divided into numerous sections, which were colored in various hues, and numbered consecutively. When we stopped in front of the mildewed young man's game, the Agent surveyed the chart a moment, then reached down in his vest-pocket, drew forth a quarter, carefully deposited it upon the red section marked '7,' and astonished the mild-eyed attendant by saying: 'My friend, just roll the wheel once for that, please.' He thought it was a roulette layout. Then we struck a folding-bed exhibit, and the Agent began to toy with a small model to see how it worked.   A granger came up while he was at it, regarded the Agent and the model curiously for a moment or two, and then remarked: 'That thing don't look like it's long enough for a man.'  The Agent gave him a hard look, and answered: 'No, this one is only a bluff—you'll find a man's size over there.   They cost s'dollars apiece;' at which the granger pondered, and went his way."

*  *
*

Here the Agent alighted from the scales, with the remark that he had gained just five pounds in weight in thirty-six hours.   As his pockets bulged suspiciously, the Club searched him, and unearthed four pounds and a half of the results of his visit to the Exposition.    They brought forth six packages of baking-powder, seven yeast-cakes, eight bottles of different patent-medicine samples, three bricks of gummy red pop-corn, nine cakes of soap (laundry and toilet), two pin-cushions of vegetable ivory, eight hundred and ninety-two different business cards, and ninety-three circulars.   After this, the Agent was lifted upon the scales again, and it was found that he had regained his normal weight.   The Club adjourned, after administering a reprimand.

# XXII.

SHOCKED BY A NEW INVENTION—The Delicate Nerves of the Agent Are Given a Terrible Whirl—In Front of a Letter-Slide—Harry Phillips and the Ball Crank—Kenward Philp's Box—Gus Williams Recites—"A Common Chord"—"The Queen of Hearts" —Popular Songs—Booth's Stature—Charlie Gardner in the Barber-Shop—"May-Beer."

"I'm just a bit nervous to-night," said the Agent, as the members of the Turnover Club gathered in the Usual Resort last evening, to attend the regular weekly meeting. "Just give me a galley proof of a brandy and soda, will you, please?" to the Purveyor; "I seem to have entirely lost the use of my nerves. All of this goes to remind me that sporting life is a great life, if you live close up to it, as we have already decided. I was up this afternoon to call on a friend of mine who is a contractor, and I experienced a terrible shock. His office, you know, is on the fourth floor of one of these behemoth down-town buildings, and between the two elevators is one of the new glass chutes for letters and papers, running from the top floor to the mail-box in the hallway below. I agitated the annunciator, and was waiting to go down in the elevator, when a man on the top floor mailed a letter and a paper. As they shot by me on their downward career, I dodged away from the streak of white, and involuntarily started to apologize before I realized what was up, or rather, what was down. I tell you it was a terrible ordeal for a man as nervous as I was! Just give me another sample copy of that bracer. Thanks."

"I suppose we will have our old friend 'Hanky Panky' Johnson with us again next week," put in the Manager. "He manages Mestayer's 'We, Us & Co.,' which plays at the Chicago Opera House; and Harry Phillips, his great chum, will be here with him, to prepare for the opening of 'A Crazy Patch,' at the same theater. Harry was telling me, not long ago, about one of those 'know-all' fellows who invariably listen to conversations between strangers, and volunteer information when either of the strangers hesitate over a point. It was in a Pullman sleeper that Harry struck him. Harry was chatting with Jesse Williams, the orchestra conductor, about the new opera by Charlie Hoyt and Fred Solomon, which is called 'The Maid and the Moonshiner.' After asking about the merits of Hoyt's libretto, and obtaining Williams' verdict, Harry inquired: 'How was the score?' As Williams is something of a composer himself, he naturally felt some delicacy in answering, and, as he hesitated, the 'know-all,' who was sitting in the seat just behind them, leaned forward and volunteered: 'Thirteen to three in favor of Chicago.' Curtain!"

\* \*
\*

"Hearing some recent stories about poor Kenward Philp, the newspaper man, who is said to have been the author of the famous, or infamous, Morey letter of the Garfield campaign, and who died recently, reminded me of a couple of fables that our friend Will McConnell told me about him," said the Agent. "When Will was managing the Brooklyn Theater, Philp was doing the dramatic work for the New York *Morning Journal*, and whenever Will gave him passes, he was very careful to write across the back of them: 'Not to be exchanged for drinks.' One week, there happened to be a very queer attraction playing at the theater, and Will begged

Philp to give him a good notice. The next morning, the *Journal* came out with a very fulsome article, praising the show to the skies, and winding up with, 'And this notice ought to be worth a box.' In the afternoon, Philp came around to the theater to ask if he was to get the box referred to. 'Certainly,' replied McConnell. Then Philp said he desired to have a few friends occupy it with him, and Will immediately instructed the door-keeper to pass in any friends whom Mr. Philp might bring or send to the door. When Will returned to the theater from a run over to New York, that evening, he found the foyer and aisles leading to Philp's box filled with a mass of humanity, and the door-keeper said that Philp had already passed in ninety-three friends on the strength of his introduction. But it was the biggest house of the week, and Will forgave him."

*
* *

"We had a little session the other evening with Gus Williams, the well-known German dialect comedian," remarked the Reporter, "and he gave us a very pretty little recitation. He said he could not tell the author of it, but he had picked it up because it was so effective. You know Gus is at home in the pathetic as well as the humorous, and he rendered it splendidly. He gave me a copy of it to-day, in his own type-writing, and I will try to read it. Here goes:

"A COMMON CHORD.

"The Rappahannock's stately tide, aglow with sunset light,
  Came sweeping down between the hills that hemmed its gather-
    ing might;
  From one side rose the Stafford slopes, and on the other shore
  The Spottsylvania meadows lay, with oak groves scattered o'er.
  Hushed were the sounds of busy day; the brooding air was
    hushed,
  Save by the rapid-flowing stream that chanted as it rushed.

O'er mead and gently sloping hills, on either side the stream,
The white tents of the soldiers caught the sun's departing gleam;
On Spottsylvania's slopes, the Blue—on Stafford's hills, the Gray;
Between them, like an unsheathed sword, the glittering river lay.
Hark! Suddenly a Union band, far down the stream, sends forth
The strains of ' Hail Columbia,' the pæan of the North.
The tents are parted; silent throngs of soldiers, worn and grim,
Stand forth upon the dusky slopes to hear the martial hymn.
So clear and quiet was the night, that to the farthest bound
Of either camp was borne the swell of sweet, triumphant sound;
And when the last note died away, from distant post to post,
A shout like thunder of the tide rolled through the Fed'ral host.
Then straightway from the other shore there rose an answering
    strain—
' The Bonnie Blue Flag ' came floating down the slope and o'er
    the plain;
And then the boys in gray sent back our cheer across the tide—
A mighty shout, that rent the air and echoed far and wide.
' Star-Spangled Banner!' we replied; they answered, ' Boys in
    Gray!'
While cheer on cheer rolled through the dusk, and faintly died
    away.
Deeply the gloom had gathered, and all the stars had come,
When the Union band began to play the notes of ' Home, Sweet
    Home.'
Slowly and softly breathed the chords, and utter silence fell
Over the valley and the hills, on Blue and Gray as well—
Now rolling and now sinking low, now tremulous, now strong,
The leader's cornet played the air of the beautiful old song;
And rich and mellow horn and bass joined in the flowing
    chords,
So voice-like that they scarcely lacked the charm of spoken
    words.
Then what a cheer from armies both, with faces to the stars !
And tears were shed, and prayers were said, upon the field of
    Mars.
The Southern band caught up the strain, and we who could sing,
    sang;
Oh, what a glorious hymn of home across the river rang!
We thought of loved ones far away, of scenes we'd left behind—

The low-roofed farm-house neath the elm that murmured in the
    wind;
The children standing at the gate, the dear wife at the door;
The dusty sunlight as it played upon the old barn-floor.
Oh! Loud and long the cheer we raised, and caught it up until
The dear, familiar strain had died away, from hill to hill;
Then to our cots of straw we stole, and dreamed, the live-long
    night,
Of 'Home, Sweet Home,' so far away—peace-walled, and still,
    and white."

                         \* \*
                          \*

"You're just right about Gus Williams being clever in
pathetic recitations," interjected the Actor. "I once
heard him recite a little poem called 'The Queen of
Hearts,' and I made him teach it to me afterward. I
don't think I've forgotten it, and I'll try and give it to
you. It runs something like this—and it is supposed to
be an old gambler's soliloquy on a dirty card:

  "Mud-stained and torn, upon the side-walk lying,
     Stripped of the beauty of your regal parts,
  Yet still the old whirl of fortune's wheel defying,
     I find this morn—the tattered queen of hearts.

  "Where now (I wonder) are your old companions,
     The fifty-one inseparable friends—
  In beer-saloons, or Rocky Mountain canons,
     At sea, or at the earth's remotest ends?

  "Like Israel's tribe, they're tossed about and scattered;
     Even the very kings might prove unclean.
  But you, old queen of hearts, tho' mud-bespattered—
     Every moment prove yourself a queen.

  "Who knows but sometimes jeweled fingers shuffled
     The pack in which you held a solid place;
  Who, what placid tempers you have ruffled,
     At whist, by trumping an obtrusive ace.

  "And when the higher honors all were hoarded,
     And you were queen indeed of all the pack,

How proudly did you take the last trick boarded!
How like a woman did you win the Jack!

" And then, how fondly was your face regarded.
By him who first beheld the crimson blush
Of you, when he had doubtingly discarded
A spade, and drawn to hearts to ' fill a flush.'

" And then they say that cards are evil's marrow,
And card-players sometimes commit a sin;
But you, old girl—yes, you, when turned to faro,
You sometimes caused 'a stack of blues' to win.

" I might recall the evenings blithe and merry
We passed beneath the sparkling chandelier;
You played high up, with *rouge et noir* and sherry,
But you dropped at last to pinochle and beer.

"And then, ah ! well, no sermon need I utter—
Enough to know you lost your winning arts,
And poor and helpless sank into the gutter,
Like many another luckless queen of hearts."

\* \*
\*

"Speaking of poetry," put in the Reporter, after the
applause had subsided, "reminds me that I am quite a
poet and song-writer myself.   I was over this afternoon
to write a local verse for Edwin Booth's topical song in
' Hamlet.'   Talking about these modern songs, by the
way, calls to my mind the idiotic words I have heard
lately in modern music.   You know, of course, that the
song-and-dance ditties are almost all alike.   There's
usually a ' maiden in the dell,' who is loafing around ' in
the gloaming,' or at least in that particular portion of the
day.   Then, in the chorus, the chances are that ' she's all
the world ' to somebody, and ' sweeter than the honey
from the bee;' and the writer finally winds matters up by
locating her ' where the golden lilies cluster'—but I do
not believe that the average song-and-dance man could
tell a golden lily from a spade flush.   Then they persist -

in singing about girls with 'starry eyes' and 'wavy hair,' and about her 'looking over the sea,' when the chances are that she lives over on the West Side, and has never seen a body of salt water larger than a bath-tub. I tell you, boys, the amount of deceit and decrepit grammar crowded into one of those 'sailing' ballads is something shameful."

\*\*\*

"I went over to see Booth in 'Richelieu' last Monday night," said the Actor, "and I was obliged to stand on a cuspidor away back in the foyer, catching a glimpse of him occasionally as some woman moved her head. I guess it was great—at least, I heard everyone say so as they went out between the acts to change their breaths. Two fellows came out after the fourth act, and one of them remarked that it was a pity that Booth was not taller. 'Taller!' echoed his companion, gazing at him with contempt; 'why, he was forty feet high to me in that curse scene—what more do you want?' And the first speaker wilted at once, and paid the penalty of his folly with a plugged quarter."

\*\*\*

"I met our old friend Charlie Gardner, the German comedian, the other day," remarked the Agent. "He is another of the fortunate people who are to summer in Chicago. Told me of a funny experience he had in an Eastern town last season. The barber-shop at the hotel where he was stopping was approached through the bar of the hostelry. One morning, Charlie went in for a shave. When he mounted the chair, there were a number of sitters waiting their turn and reading barber-shop literature. One of these, an old Reuben from the backwoods, varied the monotony of the long wait by repeated trips to the bar; and when he finally sat down in the chair next to Charlie's, and asked for a shave, he was pretty middling full.  When the barber had scraped his face, he jacked him up straight in the chair, ran his hand through the dusty hair, and asked: 'Will you have bay-rum or water?' The old party opened his eyes sleepily, and replied: 'Well, if it's all the same to you, I'll have a glass of beer.'"

\*\*\*

"What am I bid for May beer?" queried the Purveyor. "There is quite a bulge on June cocktails, and I fear a corner, but May beer appears to be steady.  The visible supply seems ample, but it may decrease very materially before the Agent gets through with it.  I will post the quotations at to-morrow's opening, and I don't think there will be any sold on the curb.  Good-night, all."

# CHAPTER XXIII.

As the members of the Turnover Club filed into the Usual Resort last evening, to attend the regular weekly meeting, it was noticed that the Reporter looked particularly glum about something. "Oh, I'll be all right in a day or two," he replied, when questioned as to the deep gloom surrounding him. "My wife didn't know any better, and you can't blame her; she meant well. You know she had been begging me to quit smoking cigarettes; but I had as many as three cells of one lung left, and I found it exceedingly hard to give up such a pleasant method of suicide. Of course, I realized that sooner or later they would fetch me—either I would kill myself with them, or be slain by some man in whose presence I smoked the little 'coffin-tacks'—and so I finally yielded, and started in on a corn-cob pipe at home, and five-cent cigars abroad. With the cigarettes selling at two for a cent, my wife thought that a nickel was too much money to spend for a single cigar; so she resolved to surprise me on my birthday. She succeeded beyond her wildest expectations. Like all women, she religiously peruses all of the bargain advertisements in the Sunday papers; and in one of them last Sunday she noticed an advertisement calling attention to cigars, in

14 (209)

boxes of fifty, at sixty-five cents per box. Cheap enough, wasn't it? So she thought. Resolved that I was unduly extravagant in paying five cents for a cigar when I could get half a hundred for thirteen times that amount, she bought me a box of these bargain-counter torches.

"Need I say more?" asked the pale, wan Reporter. "Is not my troubled expression fully explained by this explanation? The cigars looked all right in the box, and after dinner I settled myself in my easy-chair to enjoy a siesta, such as you read about in novels. My suspicions were first aroused when I bit off the end of the cigar I had selected from the box—it crumbled. A lighted match at one end of it, and my combined lung-power at the other end of it, failed to produce anything like a conflagration in the alleged fragrant weed. Then I tunneled it with a knitting-needle, and met with better success in the next draw. Clouds of smoke filled the room, and the baby regarded me reproachfully, and commenced to wail pitifully. My economical wife opened the window and leaned far out into the night. Large flakes of plastering fell from the ceiling, and great beads of cold sweat formed in columns of fours upon my forehead, and took up a line of march toward my neck. Finally, when I could stand it no longer, I cast the weed into the street. Vehicles drove around the block to avoid the remains. My wife went to my overcoat, fished out of the pocket an old and weather-beaten cigarette, and handed it to me. 'Light that,' she said; 'even that would be a relief.' This morning she buried the remainder of her purchase in the bowels of the back yard. Come up and take dinner with me next Sunday, and I'll dig 'em up."

After the Reporter's kind invitation had been declined, with the usual ceremonies, the Purveyor astonished all hands by inviting them to partake of a freshly imported beverage known as a "Remsen cooler." It was a draught, he said, which had been recently brought back from Cohasset, Mass., by the Proprietor, and its inventor was William H. Crane, the popular comedian, who had already filed his application for a copyright. All hands, excepting the Manager, accepted the Purveyor's kind and unexpected invitation; and he, too, fell into line after he had ascertained that there was no clause in the average insurance policy which excluded death by poisoning. Then the members propped themselves up against the mahogany, and closely watched the construction of the new beverage, two of which were made at a time. First, two deep and slender glasses were stood upon the bar; then the Purveyor took a keen-edged knife and chased the rind off of a lemon, in both an inspiring and spiral manner. This spiral was separated in the middle with the knife, and a snaky piece of lemon-peel found its uncertain way into each glass. Three small lumps of ice followed suit; and also into each glass went what is technically known as a "jigger" of negro gin. A small bottle of Delatour soda then lent its aid, and filled the glasses. The decoction was agitated with a slender spoon, and was then ready for the palate. When every member had been duly provided for, the signal to fire was given, and there was the old, familiar gurgle, followed by the highly appreciative and long-drawn-out "Ah–h–h–h!" The "Remsen cooler" had scored an immense hit on the occasion of its first production in Chicago; and it will doubtless be played to "standing-room only" during the hot months.

"Our old friend Ned Walsh, of the Union News Company, turned up down-town, the other day, with a sample copy of a new puzzle which is surely destined to produce more gray hairs than the famous 'pigs in clover' affair." This from the Professor. "It consists of a small, square, shallow box, fitted with a glass top, which is firmly fixed in place. Through the glass is seen a spider's web. In the center, is the spider; and, in the back of the make-believe insect, is a small depression. In two corners of the box are round, red spots, and in the other two corners round, blue spots. Small checkers of felt—two blue and two red—are on this painted surface, also a good-sized globule of lively mercury. The puzzle consists in getting the blue buttons on the blue spots, the red buttons on the red spots, and the globule of mercury in the center depression on the spider's back. This is accomplished by using the mercury as a pusher to place the buttons; but the elusive, silvery substance persists in breaking into numerous small globules, and chasing around in the box on its own hook. A steady hand and a quick eye can do the work; but the hand must be very steady, and the eye very quick."

* *
*

During the entire session the Agent had been disconsolately nursing a lump on the back of his head, just abaft the right ear, the contusion in question being about the size and general contour of a dark-red billiard-ball. When asked what caused this serious enlargement, he stated that his foot had encountered a canary-colored banana-peel on a North Side stone sidewalk, and he had subsequently stooped down to ascertain what the matter was. Of course it had been just his luck to stoop the wrong way, and too suddenly, too, hence the knob on the rear of his cranium. As he lay groaning upon the pavement, vainly endeavoring to collect his wits and two dollars which a friend owed him, a couple of small boys had trotted up, and one of them had said to him: "Say, mister, will you please do that again?—my little brother didn't see it." This was too much, under the trying circumstances, he said; and he arose to depart, when his other foot struck the same, identical banana-peel, and he slid off into the gutter, bringing up with a sound thump against a huge section of water-main. This extra mishap severely bruised his shin, and a passer-by piled on the agony by casually remarking that a misguided man, who would persist in "hitting the pipe," was always sure to get the worst of it. As the Agent finished his sad tale, he pulled from his pocket a much-tangled ball of twine and calmly proceeded to unravel it, explaining that he had started in, on the morning of the day previous, to tie a knot in the string every time he took a drink. The result could be readily seen.

* * *

During this recital, the Actor had been engaged in close communion with the Proprietor. It was evidently a case of "touch," and the outcome was watched with interest by the members. Finally, the Proprietor shook his head very energetically, and the result was correctly surmised by those most interested. It appears that the Actor had applied to the Proprietor for the loan of fifty dollars. He wanted it for thirty days, and offered to give his note for it. The Proprietor agreed to take this bit of paper, provided the Actor could get a satisfactory indorsement on it, but the latter thought that, if he was good for the amount at all, he did not need an indorsement. Then he asked the Proprietor why he cared for anyone else's signature, and the Proprietor said it was merely a matter of business—the Actor might die in the mean-

time, and he wanted some security for his loan.
"You're a chump!" exclaimed the Actor, in disgusted
tones. "Who ever heard of a man dying in thirty
days?" But the Proprietor failed to see it in that
light, and the unfortunate Actor was compelled to go
around the corner and procure the necessary funds on
his watch.

\*\*\*

"Our friend, Manager Will J. Davis, is happy to-night,"
said the Reporter. "He opens the new Haymarket
Theater, and Tom Keene is helping him out. The tragedian, by the way, is in excellent health and spirits. His
manager, Ariel Barney, was telling me of a funny experience they had recently in Macon, Georgia. It was
during the continuance of the Southern Exposition at
Atlanta, and the Southern-baggage-smashers had a little
more than they could properly attend to on their hands.
After traveling all night and the best part of the day,
the Keene company finally reached Macon, only to learn,
greatly to their dismay, that, through an oversight of
these smashers, their baggage had all been left behind.
They were billed to appear there in ' Julius Cæsar,' and
there was a· big house. Barney urged Keene to play
the piece as they were, and he finally consented. An explanation was made to the audience, and it was stated
that all those present who so desired could have their
money refunded by calling at the box-office. Everyone
remained to the end, however, and there was not a single
laugh during the entire performance of ' Julius Cæsar,'
by a company attired in the modern traveling costume
of actors. You know Keene is baldheaded; but he borrowed a toupee worn by Tom Jackson, of the company,
and rendered the lines of *Marc Antony*, forcibly, in a
frock coat. Most of the others wore lawn-tennis shirts.

Joe Wheelock, who was the *Brutus*, and the man who played *Cassius*, were both bald, and they envied the star his toupee. After the first act, Harry Vance, the stage manager, who was so many years with poor John McCullough in the same capacity, happened to think that he had no knives for the murder scene. He hastily sent a messenger to the hotel for butcher-knives; but all that could be had were table-knives, consequently *Cæsar* was slain by the blade of a Yankee cutlery company, imbedded in a bone handle; but the improvised weapon got there just the same, as the saying is."

\* \*
\*

"Harry Sellers, who is here ahead of Mrs. James Brown Potter, was telling me about our old agent friends, 'Hanky Panky' Johnson and 'Jesse James' Bowers," said the Manager. "Bowers, it appears, had an uncle die recently, and he soon learned that he was one of the relatives to whom an annuity of five hundred dollars was given in the will. As it happened, both Bowers and Johnson were starting in on a New York summer in that unfortunate condition so aptly described by the expressive term 'broke;' and when 'Hanky' heard of his friend's windfall, he at once procured a small whisk-broom, and constantly followed Bowers around, brushing him continually, and waving intruders aside with, 'This is *my* friend, and you must keep away from him !' Then they learned that the five hundred dollars were to come in groups of one thousand dollars, once every two years—the first group not being due until two years hence. When 'Hanky Panky' heard this, he at once handed Bowers the whisk-broom, and said, with a disgusted air: 'Now you take this and brush me until you get the stuff—I've got to get even in some way.' "

The merry Christmas-time comes to Turnovers as well as to other mortals; and the members drew about the yule-log, and allowed the joyous spirit of the time to overspread them all, last evening, before they parted. It was a jolly crowd, indeed, and the Proprietor cheerfully volunteered to do his part by donning a white cotton-batting beard and a burnt-cork frown and appearing as Kriss Kringle. However, he would not consent to chance a descent of the chimney, as he had been but recently arrested for violating the smoke ordinance; and besides, he feared that if the members once succeeded in getting him into the chimney, they might wedge him in securely, and then burn up all of the "tabs." At this point, the Reporter begged to be excused. He explained that he was obliged to return home early and play Santa Claus for a bright-eyed little daughter of two years, and he expected he would have to spend some time in solving the problem of how to insert six feet of toys into six inches of sock. For weeks, he said, he had been carefully nursing the Santa Claus fable, and designing new verbal garments in which to clothe the pleasing juvenile lie. He expressed his willingness to wager almost any sum that when that little head touched the pillow of the crib which reposed in the shadow of the big bedstead, the said little head would be filled with a procession of wonderful visions, embracing reindeers, sleighs, and bells; and when the procession reached the reviewing stand, and the great, big eyes unclosed at early dawn, there would then and there be inaugurated one of the largest riots in history. Time was, when this little one was much younger, the Reporter remarked, that he had called her "Miss Pinkerton," because "we never sleep;" but now Morpheus reigned at early candle-light, and unless the toys usurped his throne, his little subject would bend obedient to his will, and never weep and wail to destroy reportorial rest. All of the members united in wishing that their friend, the scribe, would make a distinct hit in his rendition of the rôle of St. Nicholas, and that he might play it for many years to big houses.

# XXIV.

THE ACTOR AT THE PLAY—He Takes in a New Production, and Thinks He Has Witnessed a Millinery Store—A Daisy of a Hat—The Night Clerk's Plug—Matt Snyder and Harry Pratt—Going to Bed in the Dark—A Turnover Ball Game—Willie Hahn Quits the Mascotting Business—Billy Baxter's Back Tooth—An Onion Breath.

"Well, I have just been over to the Chicago Opera House, where I witnessed a new production," said the Actor to the other members of the Turnover Club, as he dropped into the Usual Resort, just in time to answer to roll-call, at last evening's regular meeting. "It was quite a production, too," he continued, "so far as I was able to judge. There was a prologue, and about four acts. The prologue consisted of about four ostrich-tips, and there was a lapse of a year or so between it and the first act, which was composed of a yard or two of ribbon. The interest of the work was well sustained, throughout the second and third acts, by a quantity of lace and velvet; and the *denouement* was reached in a rolling brim, comprising a sort of millinery jack-pot, in which all of the various materials stayed in. From a spectacular point of view, the production was a huge success. There did not appear to be much body to the plot, but the *tout ensemble* was very exciting, although it did wabble considerably. As I left the theater, I heard that there had been another production occupying the stage; but all that I saw during the evening was this melodramatic and spectacular triumph of millinery stagecraft. I think that if a theater has two productions in one evening, the

(219)

management should be obliged, by law, to put one of them up in the curio-halls and leave the other one down in the theatorium, to speak dimemuseumically;" and the Actor proceeded to tear off a piece of " The Flowers that Bloom in the Spring, Tra La."

*<br>* *

"I think I must have seen the performance that you missed," put in the Night Clerk, "as I was at the same theater, and I saw Robson and Crane in ' The Henrietta.' Do you see this plug hat of mine, by the way?" and he held up a battered tile which suggested March 17th. " Dave Henderson and Tom Pryor did that, and I intend to make 'em pay for a new one, if I possibly can. That is, they started this week, and it was just like this: When I reached the theater, I pushed my way through the dense throng about the door, with some difficulty, to shake hands with natty little Tommy Shea, the representative of the two comedians, and in the crush this hat of mine was brushed the wrong way in a number of spots. When I finally reached my seat, I leaned over to stow the ' dicer' away in the patent rack underneath. You know that in nearly every other theater in town you can shove hats in these racks sidewise, but at the Chicago Opera House they go in lengthwise. I didn't know this, but I know it now, to my sorrow. I shoved, and struggled, and perspired in my vain efforts to crowd this piece of head-gear in the wrong way; and when I finally ascertained the combination, and turned it, it looked like a vestibuled train does between the cars. Then I tried to play myself even by watching other people use up their hats. I wouldn't wonder a bit if Henderson and Prior get a percentage from Charlie Herrick, the hatter, on this scheme; for when I complained to Tom about it, afterward, he coolly informed

me that their theater was very high-toned, and they proposed to oblige their patrons to wear crush hats at every
performance, even if they had to crush 'em themselves.
This hat of mine received more ruffling in the crowd
when I finally left the theater; and as I started on a
quick run across the street, I slipped in the mud, and
made two cushions before I reached the opposite curb.
It was a dead heat between me and the hat, and as I
landed, at last, I heard someone say: 'Gosh! Ned, that
was a great slide!' I looked up, and there stood
Tommy Burns and Ned Williamson, the base-ball boys.
I tell you I was hot.   This tough hat is the result."

\*\*\*

"Our friend Matt Snyder, who is here at Hooley's
with 'Paul Kauvar,' has secured an absolute divorce from
his beard since he was last here with 'Harbor Lights,'
and he's had a sore throat ever since."   This from the
Agent.   "He looks more like an actor without his whiskers, and this fact occurred, the other day, to Harry
Pratt, the comedian, who was walking up State street
with Matt at the time.   'I tell you what it is, Matt,'
said Harry, 'if I walk along the street with you, people
will think that I am an actor.'   And Matt replied:
'Never mind, Harry; what do you care, so long as I
know you're not?'   It was a cruel stab, but when Matt
Snyder is given an opening by a man, that man must
look out for something in the nature of a body blow.   In
Matt's wardrobe trunks there are very many suits of that
satirical raiment known as 'kidding clothes,' and Mat-
thew is rarely without a suit of them on."

\*\*\*

"Did you ever think," broke in the Purveyor, "what
a blooming exhibition a man must make of himself when
he goes home and gropes his way up to bed in the dark?

How utterly idiotic his actions would appear, could any-one see him with his arms waving around wildly in search of a door which he knows should be there, or lashing the atmosphere with his legs in vain efforts to locate a flight of stairs which he is positive can not have escaped! This, too, when he is dead, cold sober. When he is loaded, his gyrations, if visible to the naked eye, would traverse the wildest flights of the imagination, and his movements would appeal more to the naked ear, in fact, than to the naked eye; but it would be funny enough to see a temperance advocate prowl through a dark house. Locating the key-hole in the front door with your night-key is a comparatively easy task; but, when you turn out the gas in the hall, and endeavor to steal second base, the trouble begins. You waver along toward the stairs until you begin to gain confidence, and then you push ahead more rapidly, only to be suddenly halted at the knees by a chair which you had forgotten all about. At last you strike the stairs, and carefully pick your way up to the long front hall. Here is where you pass the three-quarter pole and turn into the straight. You think it is all plain sailing, and go along confidently; but at the distance-stand, a closet-door, which had been accidentally left ajar, creases your fore-head, and you finally reach your room by the aid of the pale-blue light emitted by your profanity. Not wishing to disturb your wife, you do not light the gas, and you disrobe in the dark. You labor under the delusion that you have carefully placed your clothes on the proper chair, and when you see them the next morning on the floor, you wonder who kicked them to pieces during the night. The sock which you supposed you had carefully tucked into its corresponding shoe, you find in the arm-hole of your vest, and its mate is in the cuspidor.

When you have undressed, you put your night-gown on wrong side before, and when you have righted it, you think you know the way to the bed in the dark, and only discover your error when you attempt to climb into the alcove wash-stand. You get your bearings again, and after you run the corner of the bed half an inch into your shin, you finally crawl in between the upper sheet and a fuzzy blanket and drop off into a deep sleep. I wish I could see a man go to bed in the dark. It must be funny."

*⁎*

" Have any of you noticed the Purveyor's new limp ? " queried the Agent. " He discovered it out at the ball game between the Turnovers and the 'Paul Kauvars,' last week, and he hasn't consented to part with it since. He had no business to play base-ball, though, as all he knew of the game was how to mark up the scores on the blackboard over there; but he got a cap and a flannel shirt, and thought he could play, so he was tolerated. When he reached the grounds, he at once went out near the pitcher's box and began to dig five holes in the ground—thought the game to be played was the old one we used to call 'holey boley,' wherein the fellow into whose particular hole the ball rolls has to try and swipe one of the others with the ball. Wonder what he would have thought if Joe Ott had pasted him one, for luck, with a regulation league ball ? He insisted upon playing second base, and I tried to get Em Gross, the old Providence league catcher, to act as our back-stop, so that he could exercise his good right arm by throwing down to second. Had he ever fired the ball at the Purveyor, the latter would have resembled one of those swinging figures in a shooting gallery. He'll never play ball again, though, and I'll bet on it. The next

morning after the game he couldn't get his shoes on, and
he had to come down-town in a pair of Arctic overshoes.
Looked like Paul Boynton.  Sam Morton loaned us a
couple of fine wagon-tongue bats for the game, and the
Purveyor said he was afraid he might break one of them.
If he had, he would have had to use an ax, as he never
hit anything with his bat, excepting the wind.  Oh, he's ·
a great ball-player, he is ! "

\*  \*
\*

"Speaking of base-ball," put in the Reporter, "reminds
me that little Willie Hahn, the Chicago's mascot, has
retired from the mascotting business.  The report that
Captain Anson had employed a colored mascot made
Willie take this step.  But he has not retired from public
life, by any means.  He is now a circus clown and general tumbler, and, since his début in this line, his head
possesses all the nooks and corners of a cut-glass tumbler.  He visited one of the small circuses which have
been braiding Chicago's outskirts, some time ago, and
he was then and there fired with a consuming ambition to have a circus of his own.  When he asked the
privilege of raking up the back yard, his mother thought
that there must be something in the wind, as he would
never do it before, when asked.  Then he lugged all of
the butter-jars up out of the cellar, put boards across
them for seats, and started out to secure talent.  He
picked up half a dozen stray pups, and trained them,
and then he secured the services of a boy who can play
the fiddle, but who does not belong to the musicians'
union, to officiate as orchestra.  He asked his mother to
sew highly colored patches on his night-gown, which is
a sort of a vestibuled affair, in which the waist and the
continuations are joined.  After he had donned this, he
whitened his face in the flour-barrel, and gave the show.

He had thirty-six cents in the house, all told, and his troupe of performing dogs left about thirty-six more scents in the back yard. Little Willie will be out again as soon as the swelling goes down."

*
* *

"Our friend Professor Billy Baxter, the banjoist, had quite an experience last week," said the Agent. "An exceedingly robust back tooth had been awakening the echoes in his jaw for a day or two, and he finally decided to have it out; so he cast about for a good dentist, and found one whose sign bore the very appropriate and suggestive name of 'Leggo.' What a name for a dentist! Well, the Professor was a little timid when he first started in, and he decided, before going up to the dentist's, to walk around to Tommy Newman's place and have Tommy etherize him. He etherized him several times, with a dash of absinthe, and apollinaris on the side, and then the lamb went to the slaughter, as it were. At the first attempt, the aching tooth successfully dodged the forceps, and Leggo had to use a kindergarten crowbar to raise the molar. This operation was both delicate and painful. The Professor's favorite instrumental selection is 'Songs without Words;' but, on this particular occasion, he rendered, vocally, 'Songs with a Great Number of Words,' many of which are quite unfit for publication. At last, the tooth succumbed and came out, whereupon Leggo said: 'I have pulled your tooth.' The Professor did not seem greatly pleased at this, and he replied: 'Well, I thought you had pulled a gambling-house. I suppose now that you desire to "pull my leg;"' and he paid the charges, and wrapped up the troublesome molar to show to his friends, not necessarily for publication, but as a guarantee of good faith."

15

"I've been vainly endeavoring all the evening to assassinate this onion breath of mine," said the Agent, as he picked the last clove out of the spice dish and proceeded to nibble at it. "I was told that they were young onions, but I'll bet those I ate had gray whiskers on 'em. No one needs such a breath as they impart except the trombone player in a Wagner orchestra. It's hard to get rid of, too. At first, it is a sort of an *edition de luxe*, with elaborate illustrations; the next day, it is issued in two volumes, bound in board; and toward the latter part of the week, it is published in paper covers — sort of a cheap edition to sell on trains. Mine even goes beyond that sometimes, and gets to the Seaside Library stage. Well, it's nearly twelve o'clock, and if we don't adjourn soon, this respiration of mine is liable to break the Sabbath." So they adjourned.

The one hundredth meeting of the Turnover Club
was celebrated last evening, in the Usual Resort, with all
sorts of *éclat* and *bonhomie*, and five different brands of
beer. The original intention was to hold the cele-
bration at the Hotel Richelieu; but the Manager, who
had been appointed to arrange for, as well as settle for,
the banquet, thought that he might possibly be hungry
during the rest of the year, and he wanted to hold it at
Kohlsaat's, or some more modest place. It was finally
decided, however, that it would be most appropriate to
have the banquet take place in the Usual Resort; and
accordingly the Club caterer was instructed to arrange a
large and soul-stirring luncheon. It was announced that
admission would be by card only, and the Committee of
Arrangements proceeded to put up a job to bar out the
Agent. They did not invite him, and they issued but
fifty-two invitations to the affair. This took up all of
the cards in the full deck, and the members thought that
they were safe; but, when time was called for the first
course, the cunning and wily Agent turned up smiling
with the "joker," and subsequently occupied a front
seat. It was a most joyous gathering; and as we go to
press, we hear the merry carol of the patrol-wagon's
bell, and are unable to state whether the participants in

the affair will read the account of their banquet in the Armory or in the Central Station.

*<br>* *

The decorations of the tables were remarkably handsome. The tables were arranged in the form of a Maltese cross, though by the time the entrées were reached this arrangement was somewhat disfigured. In the center of the table was a large flagon of Worcestershire sauce, every one of which bore the signature of the author. Late in the evening, the atmosphere was all hand-painted, and the prevailing color was red. The floral pieces were very pretty. Festoons of smilax chased one another around the base-ball and horse-race ticker, and mingled with the reports of the day's sporting events in the neighboring basket. The cake of glass ice on the end of the lunch-counter was richly laden with *papier-maché* lobsters, red-flannel radishes, and tissue-paper lettuce, forming a most striking and taking *ensemble*. Each member of the Club wore a small button-hole bouquet, which the Agent vainly endeavored to call "*boutonnieres*." He only gave up attempting to pronounce the word when he found it utterly impossible to include the entire alphabet between the first and last letters. Toward morning, by the way, the Proprietor was decorated with an elaborate Marechal Niel complexion, and, taken all in all, the decorations were of the finest description.

*<br>* *

The menu was made the subject of grave and protracted discussion by the Committee. The Counsellor could suggest nothing but "soup" and "nuts." He said that he had often heard the expression "from soup to nuts" employed in referring to well-regulated banquets of all sorts, and he certainly believed they should have both—one at each end of the menu. It did not make much difference as to what went in between, so long as they had "soup" for the prologue and "nuts" for the afterpiece. When the menu cards were finally perfected, they were veritable works of art. Upon the cover was an etching of the Proprietor and the two Purveyors, couchant, with the intertwined motto, "Please pay at the bar." Upon the fly-leaf of each was printed the name of the guest, together with the amount of his tab, and a gracefully worded request to settle at once. Between the leaves was the following unique and *blasé* menu:

#### SOUP.

Clam Cocktail (with compliments).
Weiss Beer.

#### FISH.

Royal Sucker, a la Counsellor.
Edelweiss Beer.

#### ROASTS.

Every One (with no favorites).
Bock Beer.

#### GAME.

Hearts.        Woodstock Poker.        Welsh Rabbits.
Pilsener Beer.

#### ENTREES.

Theater Passes.        Expired Annuals.
Culmbacher Beer.

#### DESSERT.

Mush Pie.        Olives.        Toothpicks.
Crackers and Cheese.        Doughnuts.
Barnyard Beer.
Coffee.        Cigarettes.        Disinfectants.
The Check.
Beer.

Of course, the Proprietor was the "roast-master" of the occasion; and when he arose from his seat, at the proper time, he was greeted with both vociferous applause and a piece of pie. After one of these had subsided sufficiently, and he had removed the pieces of the other from his shirt-front, he cleared his throat, and said: "Brother Turnovers, we gather round the festive board to-night to celebrate the one hundredth meeting of our little Club." At this point, the Manager cried out, "Hear! Hear!" and the Agent misunderstood him, thinking that he said "Beer!" After the attendant excitement had subsided somewhat, and the guests had rubbed the luckless Agent against the ice-box until he was thoroughly frapped, the Proprietor resumed: "We have had many pleasant evenings together, and if we have said anything we are sorry for, we are glad of it. Upon such an auspicious occasion as this, however, I think it is meet that we hear from the various brethren present; and I wish to say right here, that unless the Agent remains in a comatose state during the progress of these exercises, I will see that he is taken out into the alley and driven into the ground with his feet toward the zenith. Now be seated, gentlemen—the opening overture;" and the Professor attuned his lyre, and received an ovation at the hands of the Agent when he started the ball a-rolling with a stirring rendition of that favorite air entitled, "Chippie, Get Your Hair Cut."

* *
*

"As the Manager is at the left of the dealer," remarked the Proprietor, "I will now call upon him to respond to the sentiment, 'The Railroad Pass vs. the Theater Pass.'" A few of the Manager's neighbors united in propping him up against the adjacent steam-coil, and after he had, with some difficulty, sighted the roast-master, he boldly started in. He declared that he had fully decided to boycott the railroads hereafter, and he sincerely hoped that his brother managers would lose no time in instructing their doorkeepers to signally sit down upon all railroad men who attempted to walk in by merely inquiring, in a casual way, "How's the house to-night?" This was wrong. "I am very glad to see," he continued, "that Brother Bob Bagley, of the Grand Opera House, has already bluffed some of these presumptuous knights of the rail, and I hope he'll continue, in this way, to get even with 'em. It reminds me of a story Bagley told me to-day, about a man whom he passed into the theater the other night to witness the performance of Herrmann, the magician. This party was slightly loaded at the time, and he appropriated a front seat. Pretty soon, the great wizard came along and asked him for the loan of a watch and chain. The man had been dozing, but when Herrmann addressed him, he pulled himself together and fumbled in his vest-pocket. Then he regarded the prestidigitateur dreamily, and said: 'Ole man, I haven't got any watch and chain with me just now, but here's the ticket, if it will do you any good;' and he produced that precious bit of paper. And now I'll sit down," concluded the Manager. "I know perfectly well that I haven't said anything about the sentiment I was to speak to, but no one ever does do that at a banquet, and I have no desire to break the record on this occasion."

*∗*

As the Proprietor arose to propose the next sentiment on the list, a tear glistened in his eye. This tear hesitated a moment, as though it was not quite sure who was "on the door," and then it shyly came forth and slid down his cheek. "I will now call upon the Agent to respond to the toast, 'Our Absent Brothers.'" His voice was choked with emotion—at least, the Proprietor said it was emotion, but the Actor declared it was Pilsener. "It would be proper," he resumed, "that this toast be drunk standing and in silence, but it is evidently impossible for the Agent to fulfill those conditions under existing circumstances. He may be drunk, but I don't think he can stand, and I am sure he can not be silent; so we will be obliged to dispense with the usual scenic effects. Will some of the brothers kindly place the speaker against the ice-box, and hook his vest-strap to the ale-faucet, so that there may be no danger of his spilling? Now, sir, you can proceed (or can try to), but please bear in mind that under the revised rules the batsman hit by a pitched ball is given his base. After this seeming lapse of ten years, we will now ring the curtain up on the first act." The Agent, who had been pulling himself together during this introduction, languidly expectorated into the wide, wide world, and murmured: "I am to talk of the absent ones, I believe; but I seem to see so many faces before me now that I do not think there can be anyone absent. Now this may be the fault of a defective vision; but any man who has successfully played the entire repertory to-night, and piled an Ossa of Edelweiss upon a Pelion of Pilsener, could not be blamed for magnifying a song-and-dance team into a Republican majority in Pennsylvania. We are all here, it seems to me; and if anyone is absent, it must be because they have failed to register since the last election. If any are away, and they are my kind of people, I'll bet they are with us in spirit" and with this concluding remark, the Agent fell into a gentle doze.

"Will some of the brothers kindly unhook the speaker and place him on file?" suggested the Proprietor. This was done, and the waiters proceeded to serve the Roman punch. It had been intended to serve this in molds of the shape and form of the Agent's head, but this idea was abandoned when it was discovered how much punch it would require. The punch was a success, however, notwithstanding the change. The two Purveyors were then called upon to give a pleasing exhibition of the difficult art of mixing drinks and making rapid change. The Senior Purveyor successfully performed the hazardous feat of concocting a rum-sour with his left hand and a gin-fizz with his right hand, while he made change at the same time with both hands and looked pleasant, changing the entire expression of his face without leaving the stain. This wonderful achievement was accomplished without the use of a net. The Junior Purveyor gave a striking example of sympathy for a customer by making a small bottle of White Seal fill six glasses. He incidentally remarked that he had a very dear old friend in Champaign, Ill., who had petitioned the City Council of that place to change its name from Champaign, Ill., to White Seal, Ill.

\*\*\*

When the Reporter left the Usual Resort to write up the minutes of this red-letter meeting from the blurred records on his cuff, the Agent had started in on soup again, and expressed his intention of playing another string. The Counsellor and the Night Clerk were deeply engaged in a heated argument as to the relative merits of the high-license and the early-closing ordinances. The Professor was fiercely remonstrating with the Actor for attempting to make an omelette in his banjo. The Manager was vainly endeavoring, with a fogged intellect, to clearly indite a pass for two.  And the Proprietor and the two Purveyors were busily engaged in preparing the check for the spread.  It was a great, large night—but wait until this morning.


THE END.

# WALTHAM

## HORSE-TIMER'S

# CHRONOGRAPH.

## ACCURATE, DURABLE, STRONG.

**FOR SALE BY ALL RETAIL JEWELERS.**

Al Hayman ☩ The Columbia ☩ Will J.Davis

MONROE AND DEARBORN STS.,
CHICAGO.

# The Leading Theatre of the City.

### MOST CONVENIENT TO THE PRINCIPAL HOTELS.

The Management will present only Prominent
Stars and the more Notable Attractions.

## CHOICE RESERVED SEATS

On sale at the News Stands of the Hotels, and at Joseph &
Fish's, 155 State Street.

*The Haymarket.*

### WILL J. DAVIS.

## WEST MADISON AND HALSTED STS.,
CHICAGO.

The largest Theatre in the City and the most
modern in all its appointments.

# THE LEADING COMBINATION HOUSE OF AMERICA.

Open every night and regular matinees from September 1st to June 15th
each year, changing attraction every week and presenting all of the popular
combinations in the country.

### THE POPULAR AND ORIGINAL HAYMARKET PRICES.

| | |
|---|---|
| Entire Gallery, benches | $ .15 |
| Entire Family Circle, reserved chairs.... | .25 |
| Entire Balcony, reserved chairs | .50 |
| Dress Circle, reserved chairs | .75 |
| Parquette Circle and Parquette, reserved chairs | 1.00 |
| Davis' Turkish Chairs, the finest ever placed in any theatre | 1.50 |

**State Street Sale: Joseph & Fish's, No. 155, and Lyon & Healy, Cor. Monroe.**

# WABASH LINE.

THE POPULAR LINE FROM

# CHICAGO TO

# KANSAS CITY

ST. LOUIS, HOT SPRINGS, ARK.,

SPRINGFIELD,

JACKSONVILLE, PEORIA,

DECATUR, QUINCY,

AND ALL POINTS WEST AND SOUTHWEST.

---

The WABASH is the only line between Chicago and St. Louis running SOLID VESTIBULE Trains composed of Wagner Palace Compartment Cars and Elegant FREE CHAIR CARS.

---

MEALS IN FAMOUS WABASH DINING CARS.

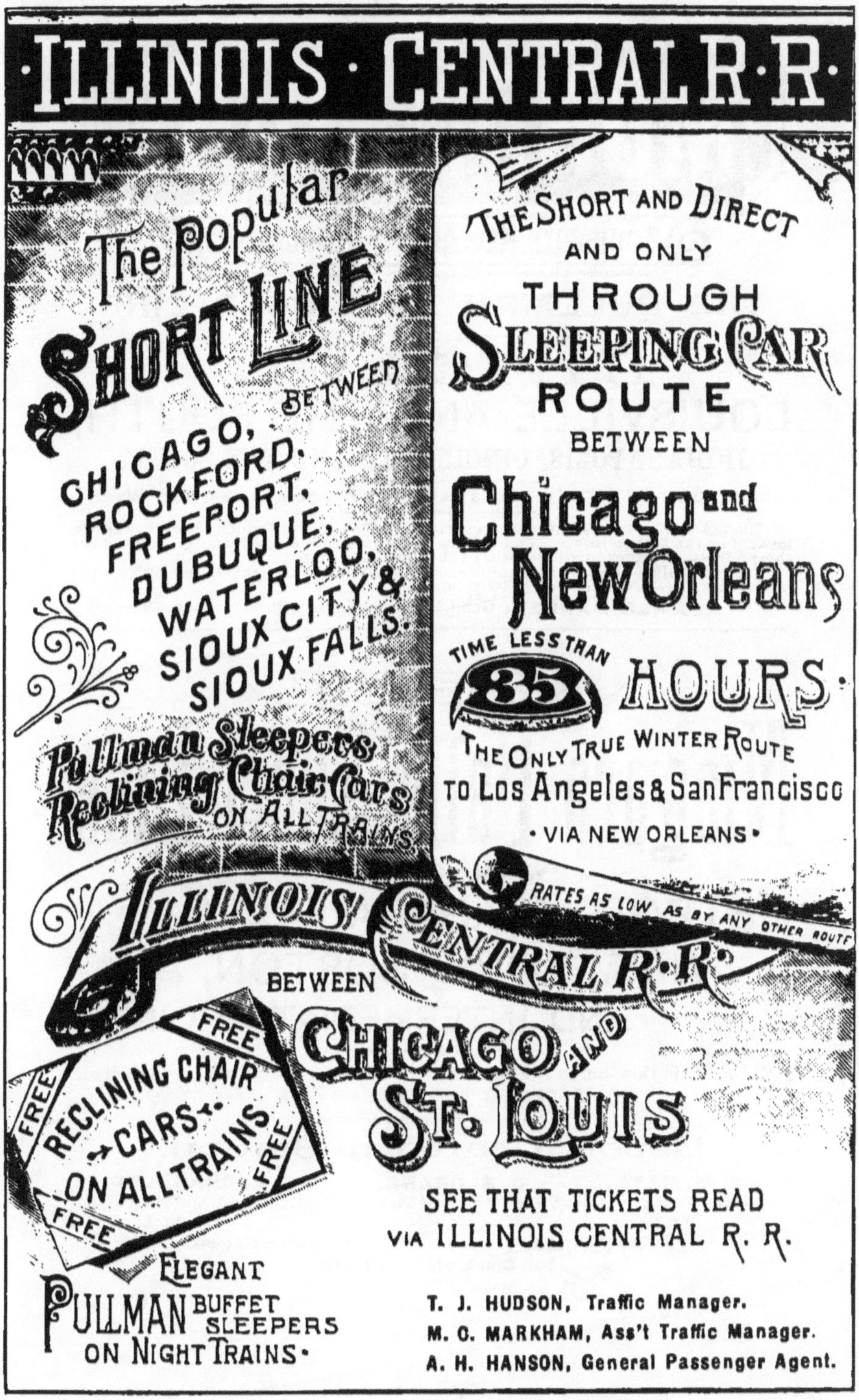
ILLINOIS CENTRAL R.R.
The Popular
SHORT LINE
BETWEEN
CHICAGO,
ROCKFORD,
FREEPORT,
DUBUQUE,
WATERLOO,
SIOUX CITY &
SIOUX FALLS.
Pullman Sleepers
Reclining Chair Cars
ON ALL TRAINS
THE SHORT AND DIRECT
AND ONLY
THROUGH
SLEEPING CAR
ROUTE
BETWEEN
Chicago and
New Orleans
TIME LESS THAN
35
HOURS.
THE ONLY TRUE WINTER ROUTE
TO Los Angeles & San Francisco
• VIA NEW ORLEANS •
RATES AS LOW AS BY ANY OTHER ROUTE
ILLINOIS CENTRAL R.R.
BETWEEN
CHICAGO AND
ST. LOUIS
FREE
RECLINING CHAIR
CARS
ON ALL TRAINS
FREE
FREE
FREE
ELEGANT
PULLMAN BUFFET SLEEPERS
ON NIGHT TRAINS.
SEE THAT TICKETS READ
VIA ILLINOIS CENTRAL R. R.
T. J. HUDSON, Traffic Manager.
M. C. MARKHAM, Ass't Traffic Manager.
A. H. HANSON, General Passenger Agent.

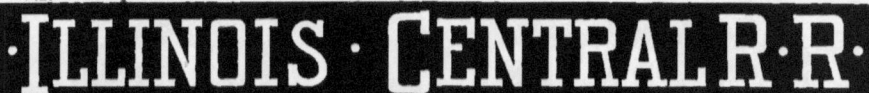

# New York Central

## AND

# Hudson River Railroad.

---

## THE ONLY 4-TRACK LINE IN THE WORLD.

---

### The Only Line Having a Depot in New York.

---

## SHORT LINE

### TO ALL NEW YORK AND NEW ENGLAND SUMMER RESORTS.

---

## ELEGANT SERVICE AND QUICK TIME.

---

**W. B. JEROME,**
Gen'l Western Pass'r Agent,
CHICAGO.

**GEO. H. DANIELS,**
General Passenger Agent,
NEW YORK.

THE

RUN

**Fast Trains** with Pullman Vestibuled Drawing Room Sleepers, Dining Cars and Coaches of latest design, between **Chicago and Milwaukee** and St. Paul and Minneapolis.

**Fast Trains** with Pullman Vestibuled Drawing Room Sleepers, Dining Cars and Coaches of latest design, between **Chicago and Milwaukee** and **Ashland and Duluth.**

**Through Pullman Vestibuled Drawing Room and Colonist Sleepers,** via the Northern Pacific Railroad, between **Chicago and Portland, Ore.**

**Convenient Trains** to and from Eastern, Western, Northern and Central Wisconsin Points, affording unequaled service to and from **Waukesha, Fond du Lac, Oshkosh, Neenah, Menasha, Chippewa Falls, Eau Claire, Hurley, Wis.,** and **Ironwood and Bessemer, Mich.**

For tickets, sleeping car reservations, time tables and other information, apply to Agents of the line, or to Ticket Agents anywhere in the United States or Canada.

S. R. AINSLIE, General Manager, MILWAUKEE, WIS.

J. M. HANNAFORD, Gen'l Traffic Mgr., ST. PAUL, MINN.

H. C. BARLOW, Traffic Manager, . MILWAUKEE, WIS.

LOUIS ECKSTEIN, Ass't Gen'l Pass'r and Tk't Agt.,
MILWAUKEE, WIS.

# CAMPING

### AND

# CAMP OUTFITS

## A Manual of Instruction for Young and Old Sportsmen.

### By G. O. SHIELDS (Coquina),

Author of "Cruisings in the Cascades," "Rustlings in the Rockies," "Hunting in the Great West," "The Battle of the Big Hole," etc.

*12mo.  200 Pages.*          *30 Illustrations.*          *Cloth, $1.25.*

---

This book contains practical points on how to dress for Hunting, Fishing, or other Camping Trips ; what to carry in the way of extra Clothing, Bedding, Provisions, Cooking Utensils, and all classes of Camp Equipage ; how to select Camp Sites ; how to make Camp Fires ; how to build Temporary Shelters ; what to do in case of Getting Lost, etc. It contains check lists of articles constituting Complete Camping Outfits ; a list of the names and addresses of Guides, in various hunting and fishing countries, and much other information of value to Campers, and which has never before been given to the public.

The instructions given are based on an experience of twenty-five years in Camping, and in the study of Camp Lore, Woodcraft, etc., and it is believed that the work will prove of great value to thousands of men and boys, who have not had such favorable opportunities for study.

The book also contains a Chapter by

### *DR. CHARLES GILBERT DAVIS, on "Camp Hygiene, Medicine and Surgery."*

### *One by COL. J. FRY LAWRENCE, on "Camp Cookery."*

### *And one by FRANK F. FRISBIE, on "The Diamond Hitch, or, How to Load a Pack Horse."*

This book should be in the library of every Sportsman, and will be sent, post-paid, on receipt of price, by

## RAND, McNALLY & CO., Publishers,

### CHICAGO and NEW YORK.

www.ingramcontent.com/pod-product-compliance
Lightning Source LLC
Chambersburg PA
CBHW030809020726
47499CB00006B/1842